# Humiliation

## Alan Horn

Humiliation

Book and Cover design by Aerophyte

ISBN: 9781973125327

First Edition: April 2017

10 9 8 7 6 5 4 3 2 1

# Chapter 1 : Katy

I woke when Master stirred. I froze, afraid any movement would rattle my chains enough to wake him. Then I remembered I didn't have chains on my wrists or ankles any more. Old habits die hard. I guess it wasn't an "Old" habit since I had only been shackled for a couple of months. I only had one chain to contend with now, the one from my collar to the track running through the house. Since my collar had a built-in electronic leash, the only reason I wore it was that Master liked the way I looked in chains. The vaunted male ego. He wanted all females restrained somehow. I wouldn't change him for the world. Most of the men I had seen since being enslaved said they thought every woman would be improved by chains. I had to admit that much of women's jewelry involved chains. More helpless, he said. I would never test it. I liked being Master's property and I would never try to escape. Being his slave was ever so much better than being "Free." Besides, I had submitted to him and sworn to be his property forever. Both of us knew I was completely serious.

My name was Katherine. He calls me Katy and I like that better. I was born Katherine Storm and now I was Katy Horn. my Master's surname. I didn't have a driver's license anymore, but I had a diplomatic passport in my new name. I was listed as Aaron Horn's wife, but we weren't married. He had asked if I wanted that when he accepted my submission, but I didn't. Marriage would spoil what we had now.

As his slave, I owed him obedience and respect. My only goal was his pleasure. His duty to me was to keep me safe and healthy. He had all the responsibility for both of us. I devoted my every waking moment to serving him. This is what a great marriage should be like but usually wasn't. So much unhappiness in the world could be avoided if men stopped listening to what their women said they wanted. We usually had no idea what that was anyway. Feminism is nonsense and just makes everyone unhappy. I used to be one until I was enslaved and learned the joys of submission.

Anyway, my chains were removed when I graduated from the training program. Slaves in training are chained to quash any hope of escape, accept their new life, and force them to focus on their training. I still had my nose ring and collar. All slaves wear these as symbols of their subjugation. I have a tag on my collar identifying me and my owner. I have to admit, It set us apart from free women. Ours were not jewelry, but real and functional. I and all the slaves I knew wore rings and sometimes bells in their nipples, clit, and labia lips. When I was naked, which was most of the time, I looked hot. Our training and decorations made all of us into extremely sexy, helpless sluts. Really, it was the only way to get to know someone well. Sex was such a joy when you realized your girl parts didn't wear out.

Our Masters decided when we girls could have sex, and our partners. When I didn't have to choose who to fuck, it became pure animal sex that delighted the body and mind.

2

All those issues of love and commitment vanished, leaving pure pleasure. It didn't matter if he was old and fat or a hunk. Or female. Of course, sometimes I just gave to a woman. It was up to my Master if I was reciprocated. My training pushed me toward a climax even when I had my face in her pussy. I didn't always get it, but often enough to hope.

I had graduated and was now "Trusted" which meant I could run away if I wanted to. But I didn't. This was the best life I had ever known. Screw freedom. Give me great sex anytime. My master was taking me on a trip tomorrow. He was visiting several countries and showing me off to some foreign leaders. The government had arranged this trip to see if having a girl like me would move these leaders into my government's corner. For me it was a chance to see more of the world and just be myself. To my government it was a chance to demonstrate what having a trained slave girl could mean for these leaders.

I watched Katy go to the bath for her morning ritual. She thought she had risen without waking me. I was awake at her first stirring. I had always been a light sleeper and it took a real effort for me to get to sleep with her in bed with me. She was great in bed and we always had an energetic romp before sleep. Since I had taken her wrist and ankle restraints off it was easier to get to sleep. It still wasn't easy.

Every clink of her chain aroused me. We slept in "Spoon" fashion with both of us facing the same direction. My arm under her neck, in contact with her collar, her tether chain laying across my bicep. Just those touches were enough to remind me the warm body snuggled into me was my property. My other arm was around her, holding her breast, my index finger through its nipple ring. Her breathing was soft and sibilant. Everything about her made me horny and it was simple exhaustion that finally let me drop off.

Her tether fell in its catenary curve from the roof track to her collar, following her into the bath, ensuring she went only where I allowed. The trolley in the track made a low swishing sound as her tether pulled it along. It was a very pleasing sound. That and the clink of the tether announced her movements throughout the house. I had removed her bells when I freed her arms and legs. That was a mistake. I enjoyed hearing her tinkling whenever she moved. I resolved to replace them before our trip. It made her slavery more real, more tangible. And, I liked the sound, quite possibly even more because she did not and it reinforced her subjugation to have no choices at all. More importantly, most of my clients, male or female, said they liked belling their slavegirls. A few told me they liked it because it made it harder for a slavegirl to go anywhere undetected.

I watched her come out of the bath. I loved her face. When I had first picked her up for the coffle march here she was like a rabbit in a trap. Her eyes darted. She was tense as a coiled

4

spring. I kept her under tight security for fear she would take off if I turned my back for a second. She was a government employee and used to taking responsibility for herself and others. Her enslavement had left her high and dry. She was not used to inactivity and suddenly she had to wait for orders to move or pee. Her mental image of herself and her integrity were shattered when she was reduced to a sex toy. All through the trek she was unsettled even while she was walking in coffle to the slave market.

I lost track of her after delivery and only met her again when I took this job at the facility. She was one of the perks. I got to take my pick of the trained girls for my personal slave. Katy was the pick of the litter. She had been completely changed by the training here. She told me the experience here had shown her she was a natural slave and happier at the feet of a strong man. She belonged there. She convinced me she believed she had been put on this earth to be my slave. So far, she had behaved exactly that way. It was the look in her eyes when she looked at me. I could see her mind empty of everything but alert readiness. She was instantly doing nothing but awaiting my command. I had her complete attention and nothing going on around her caused her gaze to waver. I had seen dogs like this, but she was a very intelligent female who was well educated and strong. It gave me such an incredible feeling of power to know I was in total control of her. I wanted to show her off to all my friends, just to bask in their envy.

She emerged from the bath looking like an angel. My cock leaped into an instant erection. She saw the sheet move and smiled, "Happy to see me, Master?"

I had to have her, now, my schedule could wait. "Katy, you've gotten a little too relaxed of late. You need a little more training. Go to the pillory and get in."

She smiled saucily and said, "I thought you'd never ask, Master."

I got up and followed her to the play room, enjoying the roll of her hips as she remembered to strut like a slave in front of me. "Now, that's what I mean. I gave you an order, not a request."

"One I'm so happy to obey, Master."

I followed her into the playroom and watched as she lay her neck and wrists in the proper slots. I lowered the sturdy oak bar, locking her in place and latched it shut. I put leather cuffs on her ankles and spread her feet wide apart, clipping chains to the cuffs to keep them spread. I got a medium sized red ball gag out of the cabinet and put it in Katy's mouth, strapping it in tight. I knew she would start to drool in minutes. The pillory was positioned close to a wall and the thick pillory structure kept her from seeing anything below her head. Playtime.

I ran my hands lightly over her body, starting with her legs. I ran my fingers up her legs, and around her hips and ass. I circled her labia, never touching her lips, but close. I watched her body twitch and shift, trying to get her most sensitive parts under my dancing fingers. Up to her wonderful breasts, hanging so exposed, so available below her body. Her every wiggle sent them bobbing and dancing beneath her so erotically. I listened to her breath whistling through her nose get shallow and rapid. She was very aroused now. I grasped her engorged nipples and rolled them in my fingers, causing a moan to escape around her gag. I kept my fingers busy, finally stroking her labia and hearing her gasp. No penetration yet. My fingers played her body yet again. Locked immobile in the pillory, I aroused her again beyond bearing, and shifting tactics, she felt the stinging blow as I spanked her rosy ass with my hard hand. Again and again my hands tormented her ass interspersed with sweet caresses of her pussy and breasts. I watched her buck and wriggle, listened to her helpless moaned and stifled pleas, as she orgasmed repeatedly, helplessly under my hands.

Punished and pleasured by her Master, the whipsawed blonde could not hold back her enforced submission as her Master's fingers and whip mercilessly imposed delicious torment on her. She screamed and pleaded for mercy then moaned in unbearable pleasure as her belly jumped and trembled with scalding heat and love juices poured in to her sex as she came again and again in an onslaught of forced orgasm.

But his motive for arousing her was not instructional. He wanted to be fully aroused himself to deliver the coup de gras and remind her he was her Master. He understood the depth of her submission and the strength of her lust and knew Katy was a full slave. He methodically switched back and fourth between pleasure and pain, not because she could discriminate between them, for he was certain that, by now, she could not, but appreciating the symmetry. When her moans sounded particularly desperate, her breathing was rapid and shallow, when she had not orgasmed in the last minute, then he moved behind her, his erection poised at the entrance of her gaping pussy, he sent his hands corkscrewing up and around her torso to fasten on her swollen breasts , fingers gripping her stiff nipples and rolling them back and forth.

Katy shuddered and gave a shrill squeal as he mercilessly thrust his huge, rigid cock deep into her. Her vagina contracted in the unstoppable spasm of an instantaneous and massive orgasm as she felt herself filled by his hard flesh. A mighty flood of love juice threatened to blow him out of her like a cork leaving a champagne bottle. He grasped her flaring hips and held himself in her as the hot liquid flowed around him and down their legs.

Clamped immovably in the pillory, she screamed her defeat and surrender as he plunged into her helpless body. Muscles spasming, hot love juice flowing around her invader, she climaxed as a true and willing slave, her hot, responsive body entirely out of her control as she submitted to his mastery.

His hands still clamped on her heaving breasts, his fingers irresistibly caressing her turgid nipples added to her passion and a second massive orgasm wrenched her body as he continued to thrust with unbelievable power, taking her all, ruthlessly. Her muffled screams of ecstasy and despair were beautiful to him. Katy bucked and squealed beneath him, unable to escape or mitigate, forced to accept and endure. He taught her the meaning of her slavery and the complete power of the Master.

Her enforced passion drove all memory from her and she couldn't believe his huge shaft reaming her out with such force. Even as she screamed for mercy into her gag, her Master forced her to surrender more deeply and fully than she had ever thought possible. Her belly erupted in raging spasms of heat as she came again and again in near a growing, reinforcing torrent of waves of fearsomely strong orgasms forcing a flood of love juices through her. She began to understand the true, awesome strength of a slave's submission to her Master. Katy shook and spasmed to the passion his ruthless taking had unleashed in her. Her scream of shock and surprise changed to a whimper in her knowledge that she was ensnared, lost in his grip, forever sentenced to be the helplessly responsive, fiercely hot, pleasure slave of her dominant Master. The captive of her own submissive lust and capable of nothing but instant obedience.

In the midst of her crystal certainty, and despite her efforts to resist, a gigantic orgasm built in her. An orgasm that she knew was her immutable submission to permanent enslavement. Her Master continued his fierce attack on her immobile, tightly clamped , and hopelessly aroused body, his own spasming shaft speared to the center of the roiling cauldron that was her belly and spewed forth his hot seed in a stream of seed, flooding her center and triggering the gigantic orgasm. Feeling the titanic forces stored in her cells ripped open by the torrent of hot semen flooding her, Katy screamed in ecstasy and surrender as she was forced into the gigantic orgasm.

Her body arched, every muscle straining at the obdurate oak, clawing in vain at the air, she arched her head and let all of her control go out of her in a long, ululating scream, muffled only slightly by the ball strapped in her mouth, as the orgasm erupted in her belly.

Katy orgasmed like a true slave, her entire body convulsing as her internal muscles contracted around the spasming invader in her belly, trying to draw him deeper and pumping love juices around him, trying to get his questing sperm close to her precious egg, with so much potential for new life.

Aaron watched her body trembling and shaking to strong internal spasms as her belly squeezed him, over and over, the intensity of her submission made clear in every jerk of her hips against him and the corded muscles of her shoulders and back straining against the solid oak that confined her so perfectly. He grinned at the enormous power of Katy's orgasm and the depth of submission it showed. His pure animal pleasure was intense, but multiplied by the Dominant's joy of total control over such a fine slave. His laugh was one of pure exultation. His cup runneth over. He had wealth, youth, health, and fortune had smiled, indeed, on him by giving him this fine, beautiful, young woman, as submissive and obedient as every man desired.

Katy heard his laugh thorough the fog of overwhelming orgasm and it carried a message both intensely sought and overwhelming in its meaning. Her belly spasmed again, in inevitable response to her realization that he had understood her helpless submission. Katy's head was filled with love and inevitable dependence. She lowered her head until her chin rested against the oak beam and she closed her eyes, content to await her Master's actions and orders. She knew she would never decide anything again.

Aaron slid from her belly and ran his hand over her soft skin, marveling at the joy it was possible for her to give. He knew he had renewed her adherence to his rules, his orders. She was totally receptive, all barriers were shattered and her obedience would be total. He removed her gag.

Katy worked her jaw and turned her head to look up at him. She knew the joy of submission, renewed.

# Chapter 2 : Lorraine

Lorraine Allen was optimistic. Nothing had ever gone badly for her. She was ambitious, beautiful, and talented. She was an accomplished model and an up and coming actress with two movies and guest spots on television. The world was her oyster. She was in Paris doing a fashion modeling job when she was spotted by King Abdullah of Jedrah. In truth, she deserved it, she knew. In one step she jumped from often photographed to above the fold famous.

Jedrah was a small kingdom but quite wealthy from its oil. The Kingdom had negotiated a lucrative contract with Royal Dutch Shell for production and marketing of their oil. Its citizens enjoyed one of the highest per capita incomes in the world. The royal family owned all the land and oil and gave every man a good living. Women were distributed a generous stipend intended to be a living wage until they could find a husband. Men were permitted several wives and most men took advantage of this custom. The people were quite fond of their situation and pleased with the Royal Family's handling of the country and its finances.

Jedrah's neighbors were understandably envious and coveted its wealth. Border skirmishes and small territorial wars occurred regularly. The kingdom maintained a sizeable, well equipped military and were good friends with the United States, who trained their military commanders and provided "Advisors" to instruct their troops.

King Abdullah was smitten with Lorraine and, successful though she was, she was swept off her feet by the gracious, powerful Abdullah. He proved to be as good a lover as a ruler. They were married in a month and she became Queen Lorraine of Jedrah. The people accepted their foreign Queen with good grace, trusting in the judgment of their King.

Lorraine, accustomed to international travel and importance in her own right, soon became bored with Jedrah and its limited opportunities for women. The King's security was tight because of the Kingdom's restive neighbors. She was always accompanied by heavy security when she left the palace. Inside she was free to do anything but there were no opportunities to shop or converse with people of her sophistication. There was nothing in the palace that held her interest. So she shopped and gossiped in Europe monthly. Her husband was generous but she had no money of her own.

Her privacy had evaporated with the wedding. Even her internet use was heavily censored and monitored to protect her from the anonymous predators that infested it. She had become a major target with her presumed political power and access to the King. In reality she had none of that, The King, steeped in his country's customs never discussed anything political, military, legal, or remotely interesting with her. After all, she was a woman. She was bored to tears and felt trapped by her greed.

Prince Ramalah, the King's younger brother had a slight build and a charming personality. Soon she was sleeping with him sporadically, more from boredom than attraction.

Ramalah came to see me in the afternoon when the King was away.

"Rama," I greeted him with a kiss, "is it safe for you to be here when the King is away?"

"There is nothing to fear, "he said, "your secretary knows I am here to get your approval for the floral arrangements for your meeting tomorrow with the Princesses."

"She knows I approved that this morning. She'll be suspicious if you stay too long."

"Lorraine, my dear, I just want you to watch a video." He held out a smartphone and pressed play.

I watched in horror it showed me on top of a man whose face could not be seen. I was on top and facing the camera. I was bouncing on his cock and I fucked him until I orgasmed. I knew it was Ramalah under me, because he was the only man who ever let me be on top. "Rama, why do you have this video?" I was terrified I knew why.

"Lorraine," he said, "do you know the penalty for an adulteress in Jedrah? Its death by impalement. There is a long, slim, pointed shaft on a pivot in the capital square. The executioner sits you on the pointy end with the shaft in your ass hole. Gravity pulls you down on the shaft until it comes out your chest. It usually takes a day for you to stop wriggling and begging for them to kill you. The crowd usually tires of the spectacle and lets you die alone. This video is enough to convict you of adultery."

"Rama," I cried, "All I ever did was love you. Why would you want to do this to me?"

"Lorraine, I am very fond of you and I would only arrange this in the direst of circumstances. I need you to do something distasteful and it was the only way I could get enough leverage to coerce your compliance."

"You seduced me for your own end? You bastard."

"Almost certainly not. My mother was married to my father when I was conceived. Adultery is almost unknown in Jedrah because of the penalties for the woman. It is only a fine for the man. We believe it is a woman's duty to be faithful to her husband. Married women who sleep with other men are considered a waste of resources and killed in the most terrible manner as a deterrent to other women who might be tempted."

"But that's so unfair."

16

"Yes, it is. It is also the law. Now let me tell you what you are going to do."

Shit and fuck. I should have studied the rules in Jedrah before I came here. I need to try something. "What do you think the King will do to you if I tell him you seduced me."

"He will be angry with me and furious with you. The video shows you having a very good time. I will get the fine prescribed by law. You will be impaled, as prescribed by law. The King cannot set the law aside for his family. He can take my official duties away, but I will remain his successor. Women are presumed to be the villain in adultery matters unless it is coerced. Now, let us stop wasting time. Here."

He handed me a small vial with a clear liquid. You will put one drop of this liquid in the King's drink, only one time a day. It doesn't matter when. You will do this until I tell you to stop. It will not kill or injure him, but it will make him tired enough that he will delegate some matters of state to me. This is important to our country or I would not have created this plan. It will enable me to ease tensions with our strongest neighbors and avert the upcoming war. Your action will save many lives."

"But won't the King's physician detect what is causing him to be so tired?"

"My problem. Just do what you are told and you may survive this crisis."

He smiled and kissed me even though I shank from him. He left me.

I stared at the vial in dismay. I would be disloyal to my husband if I obeyed Rama. I would be killed hideously if I didn't. I couldn't talk to my husband about it either or I'd be in mortal danger. I think he loved me, but....

After dinner the King and I often attended some entertainment in the capital. This night some musicians gave a performance in the palace and we had drinks after in our lounge. It was my habit to prepare the drinks, which Rama obviously knew. That day I took the vial into the lounge and put its contents into an empty bottle of bitters kept in the bar. I had no choice, so I carefully dripped one drop of the clear liquid into his drink. I felt terrible at betraying him, but I had no viable choice. The drink had no effect and we retired early. He was certainly still quite vigorous that night.

Rama and I remained lovers. I was disillusioned, but Rama's hold over me would remain whether or not Abdullah died. I needed him to keep me as his lover if not Queen. I hated my life. and didn't know how to get out of it. I was virtually a prisoner in the palace with Rama running things. He remained charming but I was not allowed out of the palace without an escort of his guards. Abdullah did grow tired and started staying abed longer and longer. after a month he only rose for an hour or so in the middle of the day. Often he was too weak to take his favored nightcap and I told Rama.

18

He dismissed it as not important. I don't know what happened to Rama's plan to take on more of the King's duties. I was never allowed any knowledge of the Kingdom's politics.

I hoped the royal physician would discover the poison but he never did. He ran tests aplenty but never found anything. I never knew if Rama had co-opted him too, or if the poison was undetectable unless one knew what to look for. In any case the King grew ever weaker.

# Chapter 3 : Adrienne

I received a call from my sister. Adrienne is two years younger than me and is following in my footsteps. She has been a model for two years now and has signed on for her first movie. A good start and almost exactly how I began. She just finished a shoot in Morocco so I invited her to visit me. I told my secretary to make arrangements for her to stay in the palace.

She arrived in early afternoon. I hadn't seen her in a year and was amazed by her beauty and grace. I was no slouch, but the improvement in her poise was dramatic. When she was still, she looked just like me. We were both natural blondes and tall. We weren't identical twins of course, but our faces were very, very close to identical. We had worn the same size clothing since I was twenty and her modeling had done wonders for her carriage and posture.

Unfortunately, she arrived when Rama was in my office. He was struck dumb as Adrienne entered. His charm vanished like smoke in the wind. He regained his poise in a moment and I introduced them. I could see the look in his eyes. I had been the recipient of that look scant months ago. He looked like a great predator eying an unsuspecting lunch. I knew Adrienne had had lovers before and considered herself worldly, but I knew the unexpected allure of a royal suitor. I would have to give her a sisterly talk on these desert wolves.

After Rama left, I said, "Adrienne, I need to warn you about Ramalah. He's the worst sort of sheikh. He thinks women are good only for making babies and he's ruthless as well as charming."

She looked at me and smiled. She said, "You're screwing him, aren't you?"

My blush gave me away instantly. Even though we're two years apart in age, we might as well have been identical twins. We both know what the other is thinking by looking at the other's face. Its almost like mind reading. We are like long married couples that can finish each other's sentences. Usually this is good. This time it was disastrous.

"Adrienne, you're right as usual, but you can't let anyone know. Adultery here is a capital offense for women. I would be executed if it was found out. Anyway, I know Rama quite well and you must stay far away from him. He took a video of us screwing and now he's blackmailing me."

I could tell she didn't fully believe me. She had a skeptical look on her face.

"Sis," she asked, "how can he blackmail you. You're the Queen and you don't have any great wealth yourself. Are you still screwing him?"

"Yes, I must or he'll expose me. I'll be executed, the King will be disgraced, and he'll only get a fine."

"A fine. That's all? , Cripes, that's so unfair. Why did you agree to marry Abdullah?"

"I love him, Sis. You have no idea how alluring becoming royalty is to a girl until its been dangled in front of you. Don't let it get you too."

 "Well, Lor, it looks like you have a pretty good setup here. A palace to live in, servants, prestige, international fame. It might be boring sometimes, but think how much better off you are than the run of the mill actress and model. I think I'd like this."

"Believe me, Adrienne, I'd trade with you if I could. I want my old life back."

"Sis, just go on a shopping trip to Paris and run into the US embassy."

"You might think so, but the US would do almost anything to keep Jedrah in their buddy column. The US Secretary of State spends as much time here as he does in England. I don't dare appeal to my country for help. They'd sedate me and ship me back here in a box."

"Lor, I don't see what I can do. If it were me, I'd tell my husband. Its his brother."

"I'm afraid its gone beyond that now. I can't tell the King without getting executed most horribly. They impale adulteresses here. They stick you up high with a pointed stick up your ass and let gravity pull you down onto it. It means hours of agony before you die."

Adrienne shuddered and said, "Do whatever it takes to avoid that. Do you have a gun?"

"No, and I've thought of that, believe me. I'll see if one of the guards will get me one."

I showed hr to her rooms and told her dinner would be in two hours so she could rest up from her trip. We'd talk more then.

I found out later that Rama had visited Adrienne before dinner and convinced her that I was being paranoid and adulteresses were just divorced as in all civilized countries. He was a consummate diplomat and quite charming. Rama started an affair with her, too, promising to make her a princess. Meanwhile he still slept with me at night. He was brazen, reckless and had the sexual stamina of an ox. He scared me. He was going too far and was going to bring me down with him. There were too many prying eyes in the palace. I knew his lust was fueled by a desire to humiliate and replace his brother. He wanted to be King.

# Chapter 4 : Caught

"Your Majesty, Minister Farouk asks for a moment of your time," said Mari, my secretary.

"Show him in, please, Mari," I said.

First Minister Farouk entered my office and I waved him to a chair. "Good morning, Minister."

"Good Morning, my Queen," he replied. "Thank you for seeing me without an appointment."

"My door is always open to you, Majid.  How may I help you?"

"My Queen, some disturbing rumors are circulating in the palace and I need to sort them out.  Some of the staff are saying you are spending too much time with Prince Ramalah. If rumors such as this suggesting an affair or dalliance between you and the Prince each the public, it would harm the King and your reputation."

I thought we had been so careful.  I should have known we'd get caught.  No one believed another was lily white, so, "Majid, Ramalah has been helping me cope with my husband's illness, but we have only a platonic relationship. We talk and play cards and board games.  He's been teaching me chess. He's been a great help to me, but there is nothing untoward happening.  In fact, he's always behaved as a perfect gentleman.  I sometimes suspect he plays for the other team"

The minister chuckled and said, "No. Prince Ramalah has enjoyed many women since he came of age.  I'm sure you know how easy it is for rumors to start.  Perhaps in the future you might invite some other people to join you when Prince Ramalah is consoling you.  It would make my job so much easier.  Thank you for clearing this matter up for me.  I'll leave you now."  He left.

Its a good thing I had experience acting.  I'm sure he knew of my affair with Rama.  I'll take his advice and ensure Mari is present when Rama is here.  I'll tell him of the First Minister's visit in private.

Salim was waiting in Minister Farouk's office when he returned.

"Any trouble?"

"No, sir.  I hid six cameras in the Queen's quarters.  You can see every part of her suite.  They are cameras 21 through 26 on your screen. They are motion and sound activated and record on this unit here, only."  Salim pointed to a small box on the Minister's desk.

"Excellent work, Salim.  Now forget you did this."

"Did what, Minister?"

"Go home and rest, Salim. You've done good work today."

"Yes, sir. Thank you, Minister."

***

I followed my Master into the minister's office. I dropped my sheet like covering at the door and knelt beside his chair. I was careful to make my pose perfect. The minister needed to know that Aaron's training made women into perfect slaves. I waited with the patience I had practiced so much. Aaron and the minister discussed many things besides the training. He seemed especially interested in the cosmetic surgery capabilities of the clinic.

I held myself motionless as I had been trained

in kneeling display position. Moving only my eyes I surveyed the room. It was refined and sumptuous with an aura of authority imbuing it. Every object in it radiated age and dignity and stability. My Master discussed the facility and me, my training and what I could do. I really didn't pay much attention. I was alert for commands and ready to spring into action, but like a well schooled hunting dog, I didn't anticipate, I patiently awaited an order. I was smiling. I was part of my position, but it was easy because I was happy. This was where I belonged. I didn't know what country we were in, but I was serving my Master. No higher purpose could a slave have.

"Katy, stand."

I quickly, but gracefully rocked back on my feet and raised myself erect. I was careful to keep my breasts thrust out, my wrists crossed behind me and pressed into my waist, my head erect, and eyes on the floor. I was ordered into a series of positions for the demonstration.

The Minister asked, "She is obedient beyond these poses?"

Master replied, "Minister, she accepts she is a natural slave and that her purpose is to serve. She also knows that she will be punished if she disobeys or breaks her rules."

"I would not like to mar her beauty with the whip. Do you have to do so often?"

"Minister, Part of her training is to teach her to orgasm to the whip. She sometimes misbehaves just so she can feel it again. The threat of the whip is not much of a deterrent. That's why I have put the control collar on her." He held out my remote to the Minister. I quailed inside, but didn't move. "The push of a button will give her a shock from mild to unconscious. Her pain lasts as long as the button is pressed. It is also a leash. If she gets to far away from me it vibrates. Further away she is shocked. The farther she gets, the worse the shock. The range is adjustable. Katy is new and still a little shy. Katy, service the Minister."

I didn't want to do this, but I had to. I started to stand up, but Master ordered, "Freeze."

I froze in place.

Master continued, "She was a little slow to comply. This is a violation. She has earned punishment. Minister, would you punish her, please. Since it was a minor violation, I suggest one of the lower settings is appropriate to her training."

I felt the sharp bite of the electric shock run through me. It hurt terribly and my arms collapsed. I landed on the floor, my hands on my neck trying to rip the stinging collar off me. I failed and lay there sobbing as the pain disappeared.

The Minister said, "Your control is a very effective punishment. That was the lowest setting. How often do you have to recharge her collar?"

My Master said, "Never. Its powered by her body heat and pressure. And the signals are encrypted so a stray radio signal won't set it off. Barring interference, its range is about a mile. It uses GPS so we can find her anywhere."

"Mr. Horn," said the Minister, "your girl is a testimonial to your taste and your methods. I don't need your services at present, but may in the future. Do you also handle pickup and delivery?"

"Of course, sir. We have Diplomat coverage. Here's my card. Contact me anytime and I'll arrange a secure communication channel to discuss your needs. Good Day. Up, Katy and dress."

I stood, covered myself with my yards of cloth, attached my veil, and stood by the door.

He walked to me and said, "Heel."

I followed him, one pace to his left and one pace behind, watching him carefully so I could follow his motion or kneel as needed.

***

My secretary entered my office. I was reviewing plans for a state visit for a neighboring country's Queen. "Yes, what is it?"

"Pardon me, your majesty, the First Minister asks to see you."

"Send him in, please."

Minister Farouk entered, looking unhappy. He said, "Pardon me your majesty. The King requests your presence."

"Of course.  Isn't messenger a little below your rank?"

"Yes, your majesty, but I was handy, and no one else need know."

I preceded him into the corridor and found two guards waiting there.

The Minister said, "The King awaits you in his private audience chamber."

"Chamber, he must be feeing better if he's out of bed?"

"Indeed," the Minister said.

I led the procession, followed by Minister Farouk and then the two guards.

A guard outside the audience chamber opened the door for us and I entered. The King was on his throne, pale, and looked both sad and angry.  My heart dropped as I saw Rama sitting at a table in front of the King. I bowed and said, "You are looking well, my King."

The King said, I am feeling better, my Queen."

Minister Farouk pulled out the chair next to Rama and said, "Please sit here, Majesty.  I have a video to show."

I sat down.

The Minister said to thin air, "Start it."

A wall mounted screen to my right, beyond Rama, lit up and a video taken without my knowledge in my bedroom showed Rama and I naked in my bed, talking. We discussed how much of the potion I had left, how much the King had received and his condition. Then he pushed my down and mounted me. I was humiliated to have my husband and the minister see the noisy orgasm his brother gave me.

When my cries had died down to moans, the Minister said, "Enough." The screen went dark.

The Minister said to the King, "Highness, these two have poisoned you and committed adultery. I think it best if news of this not get out. Have you met the Queen's sister Adrienne yet? She is almost identical to the Queen and will make a fine replacement. I have talked to her and she is amenable to this. She looks forward to meeting you. She is a most practical and beautiful woman."

Abdullah said, "Lorraine, I loved you and yet you conspired with my traitorous brother to poison me. I cannot trust you again, so it is better if you go away. In honor of the love I felt for you, you will not die. I will see you again, but you will not be a Queen. Ramalah, You were never a brother to me. Your ambition to be King has poisoned you. You will go away also and, like Lorraine, you will not die. I will see you again, but not as my brother. The world will think you died in an accident and you will never be able to replace me. Take them away."

I was so ashamed of myself. I felt the hot tears running down my cheeks. They washed away my dreams, my accomplishments, and my status. It was a relief that my deception was over. I wondered if I would be impaled. I hope not, but everything is out of my hands now. Two guards grabbed me by my arms and took me out of the room. They frog-marched me to a nearby room, a woman injected me with something, and everything went black.


Less than a month after the conspirators had been taken away, Adrienne was dining with the King.

He said, "My dear, I am indeed sorry about your sister. She was drawn in by Ramalah's charm and cunning, but I could not let her escape unscathed. I have a duty to my people and I could never trust her again."

She replied, "I don't blame you Abdullah. Lorraine committed a crime and your were near death because of her. She deserves whatever punishment she receives."


"Partly because I loved her and maybe partly because she is you sister, I decided not to have Ramalah or her executed.

They are being punished now and may return here in a few months.  If the people I have working with them succeed, they will be reduced to my household pets."

She asked, "Pets?  Do you mean like mindless animals?"

"Oh no, my dear.  They will be as intelligent as now, just very obedient toys for us to amuse ourselves with."

"But, won't your brother still be a threat that others who wish to supplant you can use? Or have I been watching the Game of Thrones too much?"

My dear, some changes have been made so Ramalah will never be that kind of threat again?  Would you like to see what's happening to them?  I have several interesting videos."

Adrienne replied with relish, "Yes, I would.  I hope you've taken my stuck up sister down a notch or two."

"She's all the way at the bottom. Come into my office and I'll show you."

# Chapter 5 : Punishment

Six people were in the room  Two unconscious young women were strapped into barber's chairs beside each other. Looking at them were two men, one large and Caucasian, one Mediterranean, and two naked women.  One was an average size slave girl.  She was raven haired, naked and collared and her bare feet were shackled with a foot and a half of chain. Her wrists wore snug steel cuffs but were otherwise free. The other was a tall, blond slave girl.  She wore a collar and high heels, but no restraints on her limbs. Both girls had rings in their ears, nose, nipples and labia.

The shackled slave said to the white man, "Master, the dark haired one has the shortest hair. I will have to do her first then copy  the style to the blond one.  Also, her eyebrows need reduction and shaping.  Should I match the blond?"

"Yes, Marie," he said, "make them as alike in hair and makeup as possible.  I want them hairless below the neck, too. How long will you need?"

"About two hours to make sure the polish is dry."

"All right," he said, "make it so."

Marie started to work on the dark haired girl.

The white man turned to the other two and said, "These two are important to do right.  The kingdom could be a very large customer if the King is satisfied with our work. Katy, you are in charge of their training. Manuel, you are in charge of their bodies. This will be an unusual organization. Katy, you are my slave girl. Manuel is your Master, of course, yet you will determine what he will do with the girls."

He continued, "Manuel, Katy must obey you, of course. But she is my slave. She is to be whipped only for cause and she has the task of choosing what these girls will do. If there is any dispute between you two, I will decide. Katy will make a plan. The plan will be approved by me and the King. Once approved, she will tell you what is to be accomplished each day and it will be up to you to make that happen. You can do it any way you think best. I want you two to meet every morning and discuss what is to happen. Then Manuel will see to it. Katy, you will monitor their progress on the video or in person and see if Manuel can go on or they need remedial work. Is this clear?

I said, "Yes, Master." Master had told me of his plans earlier. I had worked under Manuel before and respected him as a competent, interested trainer. I thought it would work.

Manuel replied, OK."

Aaron said, "Katy, Rayna will be a challenge since she knows nothing about being a girl. The King wants both of them to feel humiliation every day of their lives. Determine what they need to become and make a plan to accomplish the transformation. Show it to me next Tuesday. You can have

Lagina as soon as Marie is finished with her. Rayna is yours as soon as the Doctor is ready to release her, about four more days. Their cells are ready and the cameras are hidden and tested. The feeds go to your work room and home. I've got to go to Admin for a couple of hours and I'll come get you then."

"Yes, Master. Next Tuesday. Can I cook tonight? I have a new recipe to try."

"Sure, I'm ready to take a chance."

"Master," she said in a playful banter, "I promise the desert will be worth the risk."

Master kissed me and left. I stayed and watched Marie work on Rayna and Lagina for a moment. I had plans to make. Master had shown me the videos of the conspirators, then Ramalah and Lorraine and of their confessions and the King's declaration of guilt. The King's instructions were to punish them and ensure they would live long lives filled with humiliation. The King assured us that he had the facilities to keep them isolated and secure. He would be responsible for showing them to trusted friends and allies. We were not to concern ourselves with anything beyond punishment and training. Master would send him our plans and regular status reports and videos of our progress.

I had only an idea of where I wanted to take them and needed to formulate a plan to get them there. First I needed to strip their natural arrogance and pride away. One was a

Prince and the other a Queen. I needed to make them feel like slaves. I would make them helpless and dependent on me and others for everything. Pain was easy. A girl's body had almost infinite ability to absorb pain without injury. We all had endurance. Pain was a part of life for girls. And I had to admit I enjoyed whipping a girl. All of us who had been through this training had learned that the feeling of power we got from watching a girl dance and moan at our feet was intoxicating. We had all been on both ends of the whip and knew the joy that came from both. These two would learn to climax to the whip and look forward to it. Of course there were many other ways to punish a girl. I would likely use all of them.

Their punishment was only step one. I had to ensure future humiliation. I'd start out with what I thought was the most humiliating thing for me then adapt as I saw how they reacted to various situations. Of course Master and the King could change my initial plans. They would likely have some creative ideas beyond mine. After all they were male and what they thought would humiliate a girl may well be different than my ideas.

I was considering several ideas for long term humiliation:

Puppy Girls: Live continually as puppy girls. Crawl, not walk. No human speech, Pee and crap in public, Oral sex only. Mix with denial of orgasm. Maybe once a month or so.

Keep them needy and aroused other times. OK that could work.

Make them famous for their great blow jobs. Give them lots of practice and something special. Make videos and put them on the internet in lots of blogs and porn sites. Make their faces known worldwide for great oral sex. Maybe.

Sex with other species. Ponies, dogs, apes, whatever. I'd use Ajax for this. Again, make their sex acts public. Let their faces become associated with animal sex. Blogs, porn sites.

Recognition. Maybe I should put a unique identifying mark on their faces so everyone can easily recognize them. A tattoo or brand on their face could work. I'll have to think about this one and get the King's permission if I want to go ahead. Of course their rings and bells might be enough. I don't think anyone else will wear these in public. A leash. I'll can put a permanent leash on their nose rings. Certainly, few women will wear a leash in public.

*** 

Ramalah was a proud, intelligent Prince of Jedrah. He was educated in England, spoke five languages, was a capable diplomat, and of great use to the Kingdom. His ambition, unfortunately overshadowed his good sense. Intelligent, ambitious men often found themselves in this situation. After all, intelligence is just a tool for the ego to wield in pursuit of its goals. He had been caught trying to replace his brother. A common enough event in the annals of royalty. Usually, the penalty is a public execution. Not this time. King Abdullah was not fond of wasting valuable resources, so he found a way to retain Ramalah's usefulness while forever removing his capability to be a threat.

The facility's clinic was able to draw upon all the resources of a superpower and its capabilities were state of the art in every field. Ramalah had had several surgeries as close together as the surgeons though safe. His transformation to female was externally perfect. She had no reproductive capability, no periods, and would never be troubled by PMS. It strained the skills of the very best surgeons and female specialists in the world, but her sexual functions were now normal for a healthy female. Arousal, intercourse and lubrication would be completely normal.

Ramalah had started slight in stature for a man which made some aspects easier for the surgeons. She would be given hormones for life, of course. When the doctors were finished she was a very pretty woman of medium height, slim waist, boyish hips, and remarkable breasts. Particular attention had been lavished on her face to eliminate hair follicles and shave her Adam's apple. It only required a few adjustments to her nose and lips and she was beautiful. She was renamed Rayna, which means "Queen" in Arabic.

Although the facility's mental specialists could have removed or dimmed Rayna's memories, the King wished her to retain them. It was a key part of her punishment for Rayna to know what was lost in her attempt at regicide. Her guilt would be continually regenerated by the undying, inevitable hope that the King would someday find a use for her knowledge, experience, and intelligence.

To my surprise I woke up in a bed. I had not expected to ever wake up again. I was weak and disoriented. It took a minute for my vision to clear enough to see the white walls and curtains. There were bandages on my head and neck. My tongue hurt and there was something in my mouth, but my lips were closed. I was thirsty. I tried to lift an arm and found It was restrained. I looked at my body. I was covered in a light coverlet and my arms lay  on it, beside my body, clasped by leather restraints. I took stock. I wriggled every separate limb and found they were stiff, but felt normal. I learned my legs were restrained under the covers. I seemed to be all right, but anesthetized, remote. There were aching spots all over my head and torso I didn't remember. The covers seemed lumpier than if they were just covering me. There must be some other equipment under them. I tried shifting my torso and my chest hurt. Had I been in an accident?

A nurse came in and took my pulse and temperature without saying a word.

My mouth was dry. I croaked, "Hewo, have I been in an asident?" I couldn't enunciate some sounds clearly. Whatever was in my mouth was keeping me from bending my tongue properly for speech and it made my tongue hurt when I spoke.

She left without saying a word or looking at my face. Strange.

Later a man in a white coat entered, followed by the same nurse. He said, "Water, please, Sally."

She put water in a paper cup and held it to my lips. They felt anesthetized too. I drank it all.

She erected a screen just below my head so I couldn't see what was happening. I felt the cover removed and cool air flow over me. I said, "Doctow, wha's wong with me. Was I in an asident?"

His voice came over the screen as I felt his fingers probing my chest and groin, "You've had extensive surgery. It all went very well and you're almost completely healed. You'll be released in a few days. I'm going to touch you in several places. Tell me when you feel something and where you feel it, please."

"Surgery? What fo' Doctow? I was in puwfec healf. Wha's wong wif my tung?"

No answer. I felt a sharp prick on my chest, just above my nipple. I yelped, "Ouch, you suck my ches with somefing shawp."

He said, "Excellent nerve response. How about this?"

I felt the same sharp pick on the side of my penis. I yelped again, "Ouch, don' do tha.'

Again, he said, "Excellent. You're fully functional and will be out of here in a few days."

"Tha's gweat Doctow. Why did I need suwgewy?

No answer. I felt the covers replaced and the nurse removed he screen. The Doctor was gone.

"Nurse, why did I have surgery?"

No answer.

"Can you release my restraints?"

No response. She left the room. Damn.

I stayed strapped in that damn bed for three more days. The nurse removed the bandages on my head and neck the next day. When I needed to go, a bedpan was shoved under me. The nurse fed me my meals. The worst hospital food ever. Some sort of bland gruel for every meal. She never answered my questions. All she did was shove spoons of gruel in my mouth. If I didn't open my mouth she just went away.

On the third day the Doctor and nurse both came into my room. He said, "Ramalah, You attempted to murder your brother, the King. He decided not to have you executed, but instead transformed so you would not be able to aspire to his position again, yet still be of use. You are now a female. Your name is Rayna. I don't expect you to believe me, so, nurse, remove her covers please."

I didn't believe him. It was not possible. This was a trick. I felt normal, not like a female, whatever that felt like.

She walked to my bed and pulled the covers off. I looked at the ceiling.

"Look at your body, Rayna," he said.

I didn't move.

He reached forward and did something painful and intense to my chest. Involuntarily I yelped and looked at his hand. I saw two large female breasts laying on my chest. Their nipples were pierced with huge gold rings. He had one ring in his hand pulling up on my breast. My Breast?

He said, "These are part of you now, and your penis has been transformed into your vagina. You can't have children, but sex will be normal for a female. This should be an interesting experience for you, Rayna. Get the mirror, please, nurse."

She wheeled a large mirror out of a closet and put it at the foot of the bed. I looked at myself. I could see the bed and a head, but not mine. I saw a raven haired girl looking at me and I saw the body of a beautiful woman. She/I had red lips and blue coloring above her/my eyes. Her/my eyelashes were long and dark. She/I had a short, feminine haircut. Her/my eyebrows were thin and arched. Her/My toenails were painted red. She/I was beautiful. It couldn't be true. It was too horrible to contemplate. They were trying to trick me. "Tha's no me. You'we pwaying some sick game. Tha's just a pictuwe."

He said, "No. That is your body after we adjusted your physical parameters. I will release your arms. Move them and explore your new reality."

A woman? No! No! No! They can't do this to me. God made me a man. I was strong. Women obeyed my strength. They couldn't take my strength, my manhood away! They couldn't. It wasn't possible. This was a trick. I will be strong. I will show them.

My arms were freed. I lifted my hands to my face. Women's hands. Small, long fingers. They looked fragile and delicate. I turned them over and saw someone had painted the long fingernails red. Oh no! Shit. My arms were thin and I saw hardly any muscles. I looked at the ceiling and saw a

44

gorgeous black haired woman. She had large, high, firm cones for breasts. I ran my hands over the, my, breasts and was surprised how sensitive they were. I had big, sensitive breasts with huge rings in the nipples.

Had they taken my manhood too? I ran my hands down, down to my groin. It was gone. Replaced by a slit. Two lips over my tunnel. It was even more sensitive than the breasts. I ran my fingers over the strange folds of skin. I remembered how powerful I had felt when I shoved my penis into a hot girl. How I pinned her to the sheets with my stiff rod. How good it felt to exert such control over a woman. Now I wondered what they had felt when my prick had so dominated them. What would I feel if a man impaled me?

I put my hands to my face and sobbed. I had never cried before. I was ashamed of my weakness, but I couldn't stop.

The Doctor said, "Rayna, you have a lot to learn. One more thing. Look at your face in the mirror."

I couldn't.

I heard a loud SMACK and felt terrible pain in my .. my.. breasts. He had slapped them. "Rayna, look at your face now."

I lowered my hands and looked in the mirror. I saw a beautiful female face, not mine. Her eyes were red and tears ran down her cheeks. I stared. Dark streaks traced the path of my tears from my eyes down my cheeks. I would have to get used to this face. If I were a man I would find her enticing. I shuddered.

"Open your mouth and stick out your tongue."

I did, curious to see what was affecting my tongue. I saw I had a stud through my tongue an inch back from the tip. A ring ran trough the stud and lay on my tongue. I reached nearly to the tip. Now I understood the depth of my shame. I had lost control of my entire body.

No. I will regain my manhood, my muscles, my strength. I would once again be a force to be respected. I needed to find out who had done this to me and force them to reverse it. I felt wetness on my face and tears in my eyes. I was crying. Oh no. I can't cry. I must be strong. But they kept flowing. I dried them with my fingers, but they kept coming. I felt so defeated, so lost. Whoever ran this place didn't understand. I didn't want to hurt anybody. I just needed them to respect me. Respect my power. Please forgive me, brother.

Two big men in camouflage gear came in the room and pulled my hands out to the sides. The nurse had some kind of hinged metal bar in her hands. Its center was two semicircles with a hinge connecting them. Each semicircle had a foot long bar in its center. Each bar had a two inch metal circle at the other end. Suddenly I saw what it was. It was a yoke. The center would close around my neck and each end would lock around a wrist. I struggled, trying to

46

escape from the men holding me. It was like trying to fight a statue. I couldn't move a wrist even a little bit. I screamed, "Let me go. I'm a Prince. You can't do this to me."

No response. The nurse closed the yoke around my neck and turned the lock. I struggled and managed to move my neck around, but couldn't get loose. The men locked my hands in the ends of the yoke and released me. Now my hands were held above my shoulders. I could twist my yoke a little, but I was helpless.

I was humiliated to be seen so helpless and naked before these strangers. The covers were removed and my legs freed. Rough hands pulled me off the bed. My legs were so weak I could barely stand. I was naked. I was suddenly alarmed. I didn't want to be taken anywhere naked. I said, "Can I have some clothes, please?"

No response.

I asked, louder, "Please. Even a criminal is entitled to clothes to cover his body."

No response.

I shouted, "Dammit. I'm a Prince. Stop what you are doing and give me some clothes."

One of the men casually raised his hand and slapped my left breast. The pain was incredible. I screamed, like the girl I now was. The shame at my helplessness and pain was almost worse than the pain. I bent at the waist trying to reach the pain and rub it or protect it. It was futile. I straightened up. The man clipped a leash onto my nose ring. I didn't protest. The pain was a warning that he could do it again, or something even worse. He turned and walked away. I leapt to follow him. If I had not, the leash would have jerked on my tender nose. That would hurt worse than the slap, I was sure.

He led me out of the room and down a hospital corridor. I saw nurses and patients and visitors looking at me as I stumbled past them. I heard laughter and comments but they didn't register. A man dressed in scrubs reached out his hand and fondled my breasts as I walked past him. I was startled and couldn't think of anything to say or do. The man holding my leash told everyone we passed that I was a new slave who had once been a man. He always got laughter and I was touched a lot. I was humiliated, but I guess that was the intent.

He led me outside. More people gawked at me. Most were dressed but there were a few naked women with chained ankles being led somewhere. The mixture of free women and slave girls was confusing. It was no surprise to see clothed women on the street. I was used to this. But to see do many naked, chained women mixed in with them was startling. Where were we that it was common to treat any women like animals?

We kept going and I was led into another building. The first building sounded like a hospital with muted doors, footsteps , and electronic beeps and chimes. This new building felt like a prison with harsh reverberations from hard surfaces, the clanging of metal doors, and the jingle of keys.

I said, "Where are you taking me. Tell me what is happening. Where am I?" I felt a sharp, stinging blow hit my naked bottom. I yelped and jumped. Hard hands grasped my arms and a man said, "No talking. Open your mouth."

I clamped my mouth shut. I felt another sharp, painful blow hit my ass. I yelped and a gag was shoved in my mouth. I had put ball gags on some of my women, the noisy ones. I had seen bit gags and ring gags in photos before. This was different. A leather covered ring went behind my teeth and held my jaw open. But it had a metal extension that stuck through my tongue ring and held my tongue down. It seemed unnecessarily complex. I felt straps tighten around my head. Damn.

The two men led me into a small room. It held a table and four chairs. They ignored this and led me to an open space and one said, "Its time to start earning your keep, Rayna. "Kneel."

I hesitated. I was sure oral sex was in my future and I didn't want to do it. The other man grabbed the yoke and held me steady. Both men were a head taller than me. I had never considered myself small at 5' 6", but these two were easily

6'4" or more. I had always been a Prince and respected. Now I was nothing but a helpless female. They were going to use me as such. The man in front of me slapped my breasts again. First my left one. The pain was terrible. I screamed like the girl I now, much to my shame. The pain rolled through me causing me to curl in on myself. All that happened was that I lifted my feet off the floor, suspended by my wrists and neck, and of course the hulk behind me, effortlessly holding me aloft. Through the pain I felt more insignificant and helpless that ever before. I was nothing to these two but a sex toy.

I lowered my legs to the floor and he hit my right breast. The pain redoubled and I screamed again. I danced and kicked my feet. When I was standing, the man released my yoke and I sank to the floor, defeated and ready to obey. Tears were rolling down my cheeks. I could feel the heat in face matching the heat in my breasts.

He opened his fly and took out his semi-rigid penis. It was much bigger than mine had ever been, even in full erection. My mouth was already held open by the gag. I raised my tear filled eyes to his. He smiled benignly and said, "Begin, slut."

I put my lips around the head of his dick and licked it. It was salty. I shoved my mouth further onto his shaft and pumped my head back and forth, going slowly further onto it. I felt it start to grow larger in my mouth. I could imagine what I looked like and felt my shame growing. My lips grew tighter around him as he swelled. I still hadn't reached my limit. I kept going deeper onto him. I felt him touch the back of my throat and he was enormous, filling me completely, He was moaning and I started too, unable to stop myself. I was mortified. And with a grunt he climaxed, filling my mouth with his hot spend. I swallowed frantically, trying to keep from choking. He pushed my head back, taking me off him. I was surprised that he tasted good. It wasn't at all what I expected, but I liked the taste. Now I was even more ashamed. I raised my eyes to his.

He was smiling and said, "Good girl. You were excellent. Now clean me."

I couldn't use my tongue, so I took him in me and sucked like crazy as I backed off him.

He put his penis back in his pants and motioned to his friend to replace him. He said, "Rayna is a first class cocksucker. See for yourself."

The second man, the one who had held me up, came around in front of me and took out his penis. He was as big as his friend. I opened my mouth and repeated my performance.

When I had finished and cleaned him, they stood me up and led me out of the room. I wondered how many calories were in a good blowjob. Maybe they wouldn't feed me after this. Even though I liked the flavor, I still wanted to die of shame. I was once a Prince. Now I had just given blowjobs to two soldiers and kind of liked it. I felt the heat rise in my face as I followed my leash. How could I have sunk so low? Is this what a natural girl felt after a blow job? Was it shaming for them? Or was it more natural. A way to show female submission to male power?

I was led a little ways into a room filled with tools. He led me to a wood and metal five pointed star, taller than me. They put my back against it and put a short stool under me so that I was centered on the star. They strapped my legs to the lower arms in several places. The yoke was removed and my arms were strapped tight to the two horizontal arms. A strap around my forehead held me to the vertical arm. He took the leash off my nose ring. They laid the star back on its support so it was maybe four feet off the floor and horizontal. I felt a smith putting chains on my wrists and ankles. I felt the hammer smashing the rivets flat on my shackles and knew my punishment was beginning. Last was a heavy collar around my neck. It wasn't riveted. It was closed snug on my neck when I felt hands doing something at the back of my neck. There was a jerk and a snapping noise, then it was done. The star was raised so I was vertical and my feet were unstrapped. The smith connected my ankle cuffs with a length of chain. I was stood on the floor and my hands locked behind me.

He took me to a workbench and locked my chain to it. He measured my waist and selected a steel belt from a rack and tried it on me. I guess he was happy with the fit. I thought it was too tight, but he didn't ask me. He held up a disk with the number 43 stamped on it. He said, "Your number is forty three. Memorize it."

I was still gagged and couldn't respond verbally, so I nodded my head.

He attached it to my collar with a pair of pliers. He locked a short chain to the back of my collar, pulled my wrists high on my back and locked them there.

He clamped the belt around my waist and riveted it shut. I was becoming familiar with the riveting process. It was comfortable, like a steel corset, tight, and obdurate. Another layer of restraint I could not remove. He called the other man over. They welded a short chain to the back ring of my collar. It dangled halfway to my waist.

The men unlocked my wrists. They measured the length of my arms and the distance between my collar and waistband. then cut two short lengths of chin and welded them to my wrist cuffs. The other end of the chains locked to the rear ring of my waistband. One of the men said, "reach both hands in front of you."

I obeyed and found I could only get each hand a foot in front of my waist. The man said," Relax your arms." Then he took hold of my right wrist and the other man took my left. They raised my hands and lowered them, checking my restricted reach. Then they raised my hands and placed them on the back of my neck. It was just possible. He released my wrists and said," put your hands behind you, palms touching."

I obeyed and one man walked behind me. I heard and felt the chain joining my hands pulled through the ring on my waistband. Soon my hands met, palm to palm at the rear ring and I heard a lock click. I learned that my wrists would meet at the small of my back when the chain was locked to my collar. Well, at least it would be more comfortable than locking my wrists to my collar. Such are the pleasures of a slave girl.

I heard the man mutter, "Good." Then he unlocked the wrist chains from the collar and pulled them through the waistband ring. Then he said, "Keep your arms relaxed." I felt him pull both wrists straight up my back until my forearms were together. He pulled them up until they hurt. Then he said, " She is pretty flexible. He pulled my chains up to my collar and locked them to the rear ring. Now my wrist cuffs were fastened together with a chain. No locks anywhere, all rivets. My hands could be fixed in three levels of restraint with a single padlock. The one lock on my body. Position One: My hands could be pulled high on my back and locked to the chain dangling from my collar. Eventually my tendons would stretch enough they could lock my hands to my collar. Position Two: Pull the chain joining my wrists up to my collar and lock it there. My wrists would be held together at the ring on my belt. Position Three: Put the lock on my collar for future use. My hands could only reach the length of the chain fastening them to the rear ring on my belt. About a foot in front of me or just high enough for my hands to be locked to my collar. The least restrictive position but still quite limiting.

I was now more helpless than I had ever been. My hands were far up my back and under tremendous strain. My collar pulled down in the back, the edge pressing into my throat. I tried to lift my hands further. But they were already as high as they would go. The smith said, "Your tendons will stretch a little and you will be more comfortable in an hour. You won't even notice it by morning." He stood me in front of a mirror. Before I saw myself I felt degraded, helpless, violated. But the slave girl I beheld in the mirror was breathtaking. I had changed from an arrogant, powerful Prince into the epitome of feminine perfection. The rings made me into the most sublime symbol of feminine submission I could imagine. I no longer was trying to look like or act like a man. I was woman. I was submissive, obedient and was what men needed to own. A man who owned me was king. They had made me just what my brother wanted.

# Chapter 6 : Rayna Punished

A dark complexioned man and a quite beautiful woman stood in front of me. He was average but she was naked except for high heels and a metal collar on her neck. She had rings just like mine dangling from her septum, nipples, labia lips and clit. She was slave too, but not restrained. He locked a chain on my collar and said, "Rayna, once Ramalah, you are a slave. I am your trainer and keeper. My word is law. You will address me as 'Master.' Will you obey me in all things?"

I was shocked. A slave? I had fallen even lower than I had thought. I was still gagged but could have nodded. Instead I shook my head, "No." What little self esteem I had demanded at least a token protest.

His response was instant. He slapped first my left cheek then backhanded my right cheek. The pain was worse than when my breasts were slapped. I saw stars for an instant and screamed. Maybe the gag made it worse?

He repeated, "Will you obey me in all things?"

It was futile to resist so I quickly nodded my head, "Yes."

"Good. This woman is your Mistress. You will obey her in all things, too" He clipped the free end of the chain onto my collar and put a leash on my nose ring. The price of resistance I guess. He turned and led me away. The woman followed me

I followed the leash. As we walked I heard her shoes clicking on the floor. The clatter of my chain on the concrete floor was also distinctive and shaming. He led me through two sets of heavy steel gates or doors. This was a prison of some sort.

I felt the tugs of my breasts and their rings swaying on my chest. They didn't sway very far, they were solidly attached. In the past, I had often wondered what a girl with large breasts felt. They must make it unpleasant to run without some form of support. I knew there were sport bras available, but they seemed barely adequate for the big breasted women I had preferred. Now I was one. Shit. Damn. Fuck. I felt them moving independently on both sides of my chest. I didn't feel any pain, just weakness, like I hadn't moved in a long time.

At last we stopped in a bleak cell. There was a thin mat on the floor and a phallus sticking out of the back wall about four feet off the floor. There was a ring above it where she locked the chain from my collar.

He said, "Your water supply is on the wall next to your tether."

I watched them walk away. I stood there a moment, unsure of what to do. The damned leash was still hanging from my nose ring. My hands were locked high on my back and useless. I couldn't reach the leash so there it would stay. I was chained to a wall in a cell made of concrete with one wall of bars. There was nothing in the cell except a thin pad on the floor. My tether was just long enough to reach the wall of bars.

I looked at the rubbery phallus shape protruding from the wall under the ring where my tethering chain was attached. It was about four feet high and big, I wondered how I could drink from it. It was obvious I was to stick it in my mouth but then what? I wanted water so I tried it. I knelt close to the wall and wrapped my mouth around it. It was a tight fit and completely filled my mouth. I sucked and nothing happened. I couldn't bite down because of the ring holding my mouth open. Finally, I got a tiny trickle of water by sucking hard and squeezing my lips around its base. I guess this was designed to strengthen my lips. Shit. The water had a flavor. I didn't recognize it but I wouldn't be surprised to find it was laden with female hormones.

The chain was heavy and my hands pulled down uncomfortably on the back of my collar. I sat down on the pad by putting my shackled arms against the wall and slowly sliding down the cold surface. The thin pad did little to soften the concrete, but at least it wasn't cold. Sitting decreased the pull of the heavy chain on my neck.

All I could see through the bars was an identical cell across a the passage. It held a girl. She was naked and chained like me. Her collar was chained to the wall, too. The only difference was her head was wrapped in a leather hood and she was not gagged. Her nose and mouth were uncovered. She was kneeling facing me, rather than sitting. Strange. Did she like that position or was she under orders. I couldn't see any gold rings anywhere. Her legs were spread very wide and she held her head high. She looked like she was meditating.

I thought about my life. Things were going well before Lorraine came into my life. She was a good lay and if I had left it at that, I would still be a Prince and a respected statesman. Now the world thought me dead and I was naked and female and chained to a wall. I wondered what the King had done with Lorraine. That could be her in front of me. I could see her and she could speak. I tried to think of some way to communicate. I wept and wished for death. I had caused this in my greed and ambition. My father would have had me killed. My brother was worse. He was going to humiliate me as long as I lived. He had made me female and a slave for all to see.

I heard a whisper, too low to understand. It was the girl in the opposite cell.

She spoke louder, "Hello. Is anyone there?" She spoke in English. God, it may be Lorraine. It sounded like her. It looked like her body. Oh God. I hope she doesn't know what they did to me.

I got up and went to the bars. I kicked my anklet against the bar. It made a loud clank.

She said, "Can you speak."

I couldn't respond. I waited for her to work out the problem.

She said, "One for yes and two for no."

I kicked the bar once.

She repeated, "Can you speak?"

Duh. This was pretty obvious, I thought. I kicked twice.

"I've been here for two weeks. Did you just arrive?"

I kicked once.

"Can you see?"

I kicked once.

"Are you a girl?"

Shit. I guess I was. I didn't like it, but I was. I kicked once.

"Are you a slave like me?"

Shit again. It looked like it. I kicked once.

"Are you fixed like me?"

Except for the gag and hood. I kicked twice.

"I know you're gagged and I'm hooded. Except for that, are we fixed the same?"

I kicked twice.

She said, "I don't understand. Well, my name's Lagina. It used to be different but they renamed me. If I don't respond to Lagina I get whipped. Did they change your name?"

I kicked once. I was glad I couldn't speak for this question. Did I want her to know I was once Rama? No. I didn't. It would be too humiliating for my former lover to know. I kicked twice, trying to tell her I was tired of the questions. She must have understood, because she said, "I hope I can see you and we can talk soon."

The woman came back to my cell in a hour or so. She was carrying a small box. She set it on the floor and said, "Stand up."

I obeyed and she pulled me to the wall and tied my leash to the wall ring so my nose was almost touching it. I felt her pull my arms together in back and tie them together with cord. She tugged and forced my elbows together until they touched, then she tied a knot. The thin cords bit into my shin and the unnatural strain made my shoulders ache. It made my arms hurt a lot. I said, "Please, that hurts a lot. Could you loosen the ropes just a little?"

She untied the leash and said, "You are here to be punished. The tie will not harm you, but will give you pain. You didn't think you'd get away without punishment for what you did, do you? Now turn around."

I turned and she fastened the back ring of my collar snug to the wall ring so I couldn't move, with my pinioned arms hard against the wall.

She took a short wooden rod out of her box. There was a hole drilled through the center and a spring clip on either end. It had a metal latch on one side of the drilled hole. She held it in front of me and asked, "Do you know what this is, Rayna?"

I shook my head no. It looked innocuous enough.

She said, "Its a nipple stretcher." I'll show you.

I shook my head "No," but she ignored me as expected.

She clipped it onto both my nipple rings. I felt the pull as it dangled below my breasts.

She picked up another part from her box. It was a "T" shaped piece of wood. She inserted the longer part into the center hole of the rod hanging between my breasts. She had to hold the catch open as she slid it in. She lifted the rod and held it level with my nipples. She pushed the thin part toward my chest. The shorter arm of the "T" rested between my breasts. She continued pushing the thin part through the rod. The latch clicked every quarter inch. My nipples were pulled away from my chest. She didn't stop until they were taut and I felt a hard pull on my nipples. It was uncomfortable, but not painful yet. The pain in my arms was much more of a concern.

She said, There, that looks perfect." She reached into her box again and took out a short whip with five or six knotted leather strips. She said, "This tiny whip was designed to be used on a girl's breasts and pussy. I've had it used on me and if hurts a lot, but doesn't damage you. I can whip you as long as I want and you'll get a little pain. But that's what you're here for. Here we go."

She raised the wicked thing and brought it down sharply on my left breast. I screamed through my gag. This was the most pain I had felt yet in this sadist's den. Thin red stripes appeared on my breast. Each one was a fresh line of pain, feeling far worse than it looked. She whipped my poor breasts a long time. When she finally stopped the tops of my breasts were a rosy dark pink. I imagine the bottoms were too. They certainly felt raw and hot like the tops. She had liberally whipped the bottoms too. I was sobbing and drooling. I felt worthless. When she stopped, she didn't release me. Instead she picked up her box and went across the passageway to Lagina, who had watched my ordeal, wide-eyed.

I stared at my extended breasts until Lagina's screams shook me out of my reverie. I looked up and saw Rayna wore a nipple stretcher like mine and the woman was fiercely whipping her breasts.

When she finally stopped, she went away, leaving Lagina and I stretched and hurting.

The woman finally returned a few hours later. Every part of my body hurt. She took off the nipple stretcher and released my collar from the wall ring. She left my elbows tied and went over to release Lagina.

I grunted, "Pweese."

She looked back at me and said, "No," and released Lagina. Her arms were left tied also. She put a bowl of food in front of each of us and said, "Feed,"

I did. I was very hungry and this tasteless glop at least filled my belly. I licked the bowl clean and waited for orders.

She said, "Get a drink."

I rose and clanked over to the wall and put my mouth around the phallus. I couldn't help but remember the two men who had used my virgin mouth. I was shamed by this water source. I knew I had to get used to it.

# Chapter 7 : Training Lagina

I woke in a cell of concrete with one wall of bars. My hands were cuffed behind me and I was naked. A man and a naked woman with a collar and rings everywhere walked to the bars. She was Caucasian and he was Mediterranean. She had on high heels. She said, "You tried to poison your husband and King. You are now a slave. Your name is now Lagina. Come out." She opened the door.

I stood and walked toward her. I asked, "Are you a slave?"

She replied, "Yes, we both are and I am your mistress. You will obey me or be punished. Address me as 'Mistress.'" This is Manuel, your Master and trainer. Those are the only terms you may use to address us.

I was led a little ways into a room filled with tools. He led me to a wood and metal five pointed star, taller than me. They put my back against it and put a short stool under me so that I was centered on the star. They strapped my legs to the lower arms in several places. A strap around my forehead held me to the vertical arm. He took the leash off my nose ring. They laid the star back on its support so it was maybe four feet off the floor and horizontal. I knew I was a slave. I expected ugly iron shackles crudely riveted on me with heavy chains joining them. Maybe just a lock but still ugly.

They were doing something different. I felt cold metal shapes encircle my wrist. Then others were tried until a perfect fit was obtained. Then the halves were joined and screwed together. I felt the bolts being tightened until there was a snap and he left it. He came back in a few minutes and did something with heat. When he was done each wrist, ankle, and my neck were clasped snugly by metal. The star was tilted vertical and my feet unstrapped. He fastened a chain between my ankles. The bright light and sizzling sound of my chain being welded in place were followed by the grinding of a power tool smoothing the weld. I was taken off the frame and my wrists locked together behind me.

The smith put a leash on my nose ring and led me to a mirror. I saw a helpless slave girl. The anklets were gleaming silver like jewelry, but much stronger. I looked carefully, but could not see a seam. My collar was just a larger version. The hobble between my ankles was not heavy. Each link shone with a burnished finish. The smith said proudly, "All your chains are fashioned from stainless steel." I could see it would be difficult and expensive to remove my chains. That was something to ponder

He led me to a workbench and locked my chain to it. He measured my waist and selected a steel belt from a rack and tried it on me. I guess he was happy with the fit. It was too tight, but he didn't ask me. He held up a disk with the number 44 stamped on it. He said, "Your number is forty four. Memorize it."

I said, "Yes, Master."

He attached it to my collar with a pair of pliers. He locked a short chain to the back of my collar, pulled my wrists high on my back and locked them there.

He clamped the belt around my waist and riveted it shut. It was comfortable, like a steel corset, tight, and obdurate. Another layer of restraint I could not remove. They welded a short chain to the back ring of my collar. Cunning metal shield were used to protect my naked body from the hot spatterings. The chain dangled above my waist

The men unlocked my wrists. They measured the length of my arms and the distance between my collar and waistband. then cut two short lengths of chin and welded them to my wrist cuffs. The other end of the chains locked to the rear ring of my waistband. One of the men said, "reach both hands in front of you."

I obeyed and found I could only get each hand a foot in front of my waist. The man said," Relax your arms." Then he took hold of my right wrist and the other man took my left. They raised my hands and lowered them, checking my restricted reach. Then they raised my hands and placed them on the back of my neck. It was just  possible. The released her wrists and said," put your hands behind you, palms touching."

I obeyed and one man walked behind me. I heard and felt the chain joining my hands pulled through the ring on my waistband. Soon my hands met, palm to palm at the rear ring and I heard a lock click. I learned that my wrists would meet at the small of my back when the chain locked to my collar. Well, at least it would be more comfortable than locking my wrists to my collar like Roseann. Such are the pleasures of even a willing slave girl.

He unlocked the wrist chains from the collar and pulled them through the waistband ring. Then he said, "Keep your arms relaxed." I felt him pull both wrists straight up my back until my forearms were together.  He pulled them up until they hurt. Then he said, " She is pretty flexible. He pulled my chains up to my collar and locked them to the rear ring. Now my wrist cuffs were fastened together with a chain. No locks anywhere, all rivets. My hands could be fixed in three levels of restraint with a single padlock. The one lock on my body. Position One: My hands could be pulled high on my back and locked to the chain dangling from my collar. Eventually my tendons would stretch enough they could lock my hands to my collar. Position Two: Pull the chain joining my wrists up to my collar and lock it there. My wrists would be held together at the ring on my belt. Position Three: Put the lock on my collar for future use. My hands could only reach the length of the chain fastening them to the rear ring on my belt. About a foot in front of me or just high enough for my hands to be locked to my collar. The least restrictive position but still quite limiting.

I was now more helpless than I had ever been. My hands were far up my back and under tremendous strain. My collar pulled down in the back, the edge pressing into my throat. I tried to lift my hands further. But they were already as high as they would go. The smith said, "Your tendons will stretch a little and you will be more comfortable in an hour. You won't even notice it by morning." The blindfold covered my eyes again. A ball gag was strapped tight in my mouth. I was led somewhere and backed up against a flat surface. A strap was tightened around my waist. Then others pulled me tight against the surface. Above my breasts and below them. A form fitting shell was placed on the back of my head then a strap around my forehead. My legs were pulled as far apart as my hobble allowed. My knees were pulled wider and strapped tight. Now I was immobile, gagged, and blindfolded. Great. I guessed I was going to be ringed now. Not my choice but I couldn't even protest. I hope they didn't hurt.

The men stroked my nipples and clit until they grew rigid. Against my will, the traitorous nipples swelled. Standing rigid at attention above my heaving breasts. ready to be forever changed.

They applied a cool liquid to my rock hard nipples and I felt the needle slide into my flesh. It was smooth and fast and felt more like a poke than the fabled prick. I felt the ring push the needle back out. I could only gasp and moan. I heard the clicking as their internal locks engaged, but I could not raise my strapped head to see. Then each of my ears received their rings. The King has gotten his wish. I'm glad he's not here to see me. I bet he's getting pictures, though. Nothing I can do about it, but I'll never be able to covet his position again. I could almost admire his cleverness if it didn't have such personal impact.

Outrage and pain colored the single scream I emitted as they pierced my clit hood. I only sobbed as they locked the ring within my secret place and my labia lips received similar rings.

At first, I raged at the violation of my body. Then I realized I was helpless to do anything about it. I knew I would be coveted by men. I wish I had some say about who took me. One of the men applied a lotion to each of my new rings and rotated them within my flesh. He did not say anything. Neither did I. They were handling me and I wanted their care. I was so helpless!

Then I felt the cool liquid spread in both nostrils. Something cold and large thrust into both nostrils. There was a sharp click and my face filled with pain. The pain was much stronger than the other piercings. It was sickening and I had

71

no defense against it. I screamed into my gag. The pain was sharp and pointed. It thrust up into my brain and made my ears hurt. I tried to shake my head but it wouldn't move at all. I felt the cold object removed from my nose but the pain didn't go away. Then I felt fingers doing something else in my nose. Something narrower slipped into my nostrils. I felt pressure squeezing my septum. There was a click and the thing left my nose, but I still felt the squeezing pressure.

I recognized what had been done to me. They had made a large hole in my septum and then put a grommet in the hole to ensure it would never grow smaller. This made the ring they planned to put in my nose free to swing. It also meant I could stand a stronger pull on my nose.

I squealed into my gag and tried to plead with the men to not ring my nose. No intelligible sound made it past the large gag, but, of course, the men understood me. I understood my opinion and desires did not matter to the men. They were just doing their job. And, undoubtedly, enjoying it.

I felt the fingers come back to my nose. I heard the locks click and felt the weight pull on my septum. and knew I was ringed, collared, and chained as a slave where everyone could see. I felt an unaccustomed weight on my lips and knew it would be the heaviest weight to bear.

I had large rings all over my body. Obviously not just for adornment. Any child who hooked a finger through any of my rings could control me, even if I wasn't chained. Shit. I

72

was such a fool. I was the proverbial 'dumb blond.' I felt drained and beyond caring. I just wanted to be left alone. I sobbed quietly in my mute darkness.

I felt a needle jab my arm and the soothing darkness enveloped me. When I awoke, I was still strapped to the wall, there was something in my mouth, and my tongue hurt. I said, "My tongue huwts." Whatever was in my mouth wasn't a gag, but distorted my words. I couldn't think of any way this could be good.

No response.

The straps holding me to the flat surface left me. I might have fallen but a hand steadied me. The blindfold and gag were removed. The light was too bright at first. When I could see again a man stood me in front of a mirror. Before I saw myself I felt degraded, helpless, violated. But the slave girl I beheld in the mirror was breathtaking. I had changed from a symbol of female power into an example of feminine perfection. The rings made me into the most sublime symbol of feminine submission I could imagine. I no longer was trying to look like or act like a man. I was woman. I was submissive, obedient and was what men needed to own. I felt the heavy weight hanging from my nose. I had been ringed. I was so violated. I was so enslaved. My King had done as he pleased with me and I could do nothing. I was a slave. I was only fit to be owned and the man who owned me was king. They had made me just what men wanted.

I looked at the large, thick rings in my body. They were over an inch in diameter and looked almost a quarter inch thick. They was smooth and looked surprisingly good. They weren't feminine. They adorned but they had another message beyond jewelry. They were something an owner would put on livestock. They had their own beauty just as anything that elegantly fitted its purpose did. The rings were intended to control me. They informed strangers that they had been placed on me without my consent. It showed the world that I was property and owned, that my opinion did not matter.

I opened my mouth and stuck out my tongue, curious to see what was affecting it. I saw I had a stud through my tongue an inch back from the tip. A ring ran trough the stud and lay on my tongue. It reached nearly to the tip. Wonderful. A ring everywhere to control me. It didn't matter. I deserved whatever the King wanted for my punishment. I was a slave girl and I had to get used to being livestock.

I felt all the heavy weights move in my flesh. It was similar to heavy earrings I had worn, but the message was so different. This was not mere adornment I had chosen. This heavy metal in my body was the hand of my master reaching out across space and time to perfect my control. I knew I would obey the slightest tug on any of them. A vision of me ardently following a leash clipped to my nose ring popped into my mind. I felt submissive arousal blossom in my loins as I gazed at myself.

A leather hood was laced around my head blocking sight and muffling sound. Only my nose and mouth were not covered.

I heard, "Open." I opened my mouth and something was carefully inserted in my mouth. I felt a flat rod slide into my tongue ring followed by a round leather something wedged behind my teeth Straps held it in place. The rod held my tongue down and the round thing kept my teeth far apart. I couldn't close my lips. It was not comfortable. I started drooling immediately and I found it hard to swallow with this thing in my mouth. The gag pushed on my tongue ring uncomfortably. A chain was locked on my collar and I heard a woman's voice say, "Follow the pull on your collar. Walk slow."

I followed the tug of my leash. I was grateful she hadn't attached it to my new tender nose ring. I felt it sway as I walked.

I was taken somewhere close by. I felt and heard my collar chain locked to something then I heard a man say, "Your water supply is on the wall under your tether. Just suck." Then I heard the naked girl leave, her heels clicking on the concrete floor.

I explored by touch and found I was tethered to a ring solidly set in a concrete wall. I found a thin mat, I guess it was my bed. I would stand and sit on it too. I felt for the water and found a male phallus shape sticking out of the wall . It was rubbery and big. I was familiar with the concept of a blow job. Poorly named since the girl was supposed to suck, not blow. I stuck it in my mouth and couldn't get any water until I had it all the way in and sucked hard. I got a trickle of cold water if I sucked hard and squeezed my lips hard around it. I found nothing else within the span of my tether. I sat on the mat and waited. When I was still I heard the soft clank of chain on concrete nearby. I wasn't alone, but whoever was with me was silent. I guessed she was gagged like me. I considered Morse code, but I only knew S and O.

 Panic threatened to engulf me as I realized how securely I was imprisoned. I called out, "Is anyone here?" But the gag made my speech unintelligible. I felt a sharp pain in my nose when I opened my mouth. Why had they put  ring in my nose? That smacked of punishment. It was something you did to humiliate a girl when you intended to keep her. It was done so that others would look down upon the girl as a slave. A former Queen now under the control of others.

I felt fine now except for being naked, chained and blind. OK I wasn't fine. What the fuck was happening to me? Why me? I also didn't know where I was or how long I had been unconscious. I wasn't starving, so no more than a day or two.

76

I stood up, cautiously and followed the wall to the end of my tether. I could only take small steps, maybe a foot before my ankle was snubbed short. Nothing. I went back the other way. Nothing. I stretched my feet out as far away from the ring as possible. Nothing. I crept around in my personal darkness, afraid of falling. Nothing. I went back to the wall. I tried to stretch my hearing and smell as far as I could. Nothing. All I had were my chains and hard concrete. The former sounds were now silent. I waited. There was nothing else to do.

A noise. I heard something. Far away. It was the sound of a man's shoes approaching. Thank God. Wait, was he here to help me? He removed my gag,

A man said, "Hello, Lagina. Not too uncomfortable, I hope?"

"Yes, I'm uncomfowtable. I'm chained to a wall. I'm naked. I'm tewified. There's something in my mouf so I can't tawk wight. Are you in chawge?"

I felt a fiery burning pain on my thigh. I screamed and a hard ball was stuffed in my mouth. I felt her hands buckle it tight in my mouth. I tried to tell her I was sorry, but the ball held my tongue down and I could only grunt. I heard his footsteps walk away." Oh No. Please don't go. Come back. I need water. Please, I silently thought.

I heard him say, "Your tongue is swollen. It will be better tomorrow," and he went away.

He didn't go far. He must have gone to the other person nearby. I heard someone talking but got no meaning from the sounds. I heard him walk away, accompanied by the sounds of chain clattering on the floor. It was very quiet after that. I guessed Master had taken the other girl away with him.

I cried for my lost freedom, my lost water, my lost sight. I pleaded with God to let me see and walk and drink again.

I slept again. I awoke to approaching footsteps. I struggled up against the wall and waited. At least my tongue felt better.

The man, I think it was the same one, said, "I'm here to give you some water. Do not speak."

I felt him remove the gag. I licked my dry lips and opened my mouth. He held a water bottle to my lips and let water run in. I bathed my tongue in it. I let it trickle down my parched throat until it was all gone. He said, "I'll bring some food later. Then we can talk. Open." He put the gag back in and fastened it. I heard his footsteps go away. It was a lonely sound.

My relentless soul searching started again. Who was he. Was he my captor? An employee? Or something else. There was so much I needed to know. I tried to focus on my questions. What was going to happen to me? Where was I? Who was in charge? Why was I hooded and gagged? Would I be raped?  I would hold that one for last.  I was sure that was my fate, otherwise why keep me naked and helpless?

He was gone a long time.  He had implied it wouldn't be a long time.  I was hungry.  Every time I thought about food, my hunger grew.  Now I was ravenous.  My stomach was growling.  I had gotten soft in my time as Queen.  Servants and slaves would hurry at my slightest wish to satisfy me.  Finally, I heard his footsteps coming.

He said, "Lagina.  I brought you some food.  I will feed you.  You may not ask questions or complain."  He removed my gag and gave me another drink.

"Get on your knees and spread them wide.  Arch your back.  Hold your head up high.  Keep your ass on your heels.  Get in this position when a mistress or master enters.  Is this clear?

"Yes." I positioned myself as he ordered. I had difficulty with my chained limbs.  I managed it eventually.  I would have done almost anything for food.

After I was kneeling he said, "Spread your legs wider. Your cunt should kiss the floor. Stick your breasts out more."

I tried.  I arched my back and spread my knees as far as I could.  I strained downwards.  I said, "This is as far as I can go."

He said, "Barely acceptable. Practice when I'm gone. Standing pose has the same posture rules. You must be able to switch back and forth with grace. Practice this too. Your cunt must kiss the floor next time, or no food. You are a slave girl. There are some rules you must obey or be punished. You may only kneel or stand during the day. You may lay down to sleep. Kneel facing the door. You may speak only if you have permission or are responding to a mistress or master. You will address me as Master. You will verbally acknowledge any order. Is this clear?"

I said, "Yes."

A searing pain erupted in my breasts. I yelped. Fucked up already. Damn.

"Yes, what, slave?"

"Yes, Master, I'm sorry," I said, "but this is cruel. Its inhuman to treat me like this. I'm helpless. Can't you be kinder? Don't you know I was a Queen. I don't know how to do these things. I've never knelt in my life."

Pain erupted in my thigh. I jumped and twisted, Crying out, "Please, I'm sorry. What did I do?" I fell back on my bottom and back, my arms and legs made useless by the chains clinking around me.

He said, "You did not ask permission to speak and complaining earns you a correction. Be quiet and get back in position."

I righted myself and knelt with my knees as wide as I could. Tears were wetting the leather on my face.

He resumed, "You once were a Queen. Now you're just a female slave being punished. You're not human now. You're just livestock. You'll be handled and trained. You'll always be chained and used as your masters and mistresses wish. You need to learn obedience and respect for your betters. And everyone is your better now."

"No," I cried, "it wasn't my fault. I was blackmailed."

Pain seared my breasts twice. I screamed but I didn't move. I was learning. I must learn to curb my tongue. Master was here to punish me and didn't care if it was just. In my heart I knew it was. I had earned punishment. It looked like I was going to get it, too. Shit.

I heard him laugh, "Hah. That doesn't matter now. Even if someone found you, Do you think your people would want a ringed slut as their Queen anymore? Your royal days are over."

He asked me a question. I had to answer. I knew I had to be careful and respectful. "Master, my people love me. They will rejoice when they see me again."

"Lagina, You've been sedated for a while and you look better than you used to. You've had a few improvements made and your people won't recognize you. Someday I might take your hood off and let you see. Right now, I am your Master. I control you. Your water, food, pain, sight and everything else about you. I am your Master and you will address me as such. You will acknowledge my every command with, 'Yes, Master,' 'No, Master,' and so forth. Do not speak without permission. Is all that clear?"

"Yes," I said, sullenly."

Pain erupted again on my breasts and I cried out, "Yes, Master. It is clear."

Master! No way in hell. A girl's breasts are just too perfect for punishment. They're sensitive and stick out in front. Just too perfect for controlling and punishing me. Did nature put them there because an obedient girl is a survival characteristic? Even if I was a prisoner, I was not a maid or a menial. I would play along until I could find out what was going on. "Yes, Master. I'm sorry, I have never been in this position before. It will take me a little while to adjust. I would be grateful if my sight could be restored and my hands and feet freed. I know I am fastened to a wall, so I could not escape."

"No." He put a piece of apple in my mouth. It was by far the best food I had ever had.

82

I ate it and opened my mouth for more. A piece of orange was put in. I sucked that down quickly, Next I got a piece of carrot, followed by broccoli.

"Master. I need to go to the bathroom soon. Could you take me?

"No. I have brought you a pail. I will put it next to the wall on your right. If you make a mess, you'll clean it up with your tongue. Be careful."

I heard him put it down. I would never know if I were being watched. To use the pail in front of unknown watchers was daunting. I don't doubt I will use the pail when need becomes urgent. The pail and hood and chains must be punishment. The insidious punishment of the hood was clear. I damned the hood and the pail and my captor. I was helpless. I wanted to cry, but the hood suppressed the tears.

"Master, this is frightening me. I don't know how long this will last."

"I would be frightened too, Lagina."

"It would be less frightening if I could see. I will pay money to get rid of the hood."

"I'm sure you would, Lagina."

"Can you tell me how long I have to wear it?"

The pain was fearful as the whip scalded my breasts. I screamed again and again. I rolled over to my side. I struggled hopelessly to touch my inflamed chest. My chains clattered again and again as I fought the unyielding links. I was more helpless than any chained animal ever was. Once again she pulled me upright. I sobbed with hopeless anguish. I was so damned helpless against this demonic woman.

"No questions Lagina. You will wear that hood until you are ready to have it removed. Maybe you will wear it for life."

"Mistress, I don't know how to get ready. I think I'll go crazy first."

"Maybe not. The whip will teach you."

"I would like to speak to whoever sets the standards for me."

The whip scalded my thigh. I screamed and rolled on the ground. My chains clattered and clanked as I tried to reach the fiery cut and sooth it. My every motion was snubbed by the unyielding links. No animal was ever as restrained as I. I sobbed into my hood.

Strong hands lifted me to my knees. He held another piece of apple to my lips. "That was a demand, Lagina."

I ate an apple and an orange, some vegetable. I was full. "Master can I know why I'm here?"

Another horribly painful blow on my back. I screamed and the gag was stuffed back into me.

"Because you are beautiful, acted badly, and someone wants you punished and trained." I heard him leave.

Because someone wants me? Punished I expected, but not training. Criminals were either executed or put in prison, not this. Wants me trained? For what? To do what? I was indignant. Some one took me and chained me naked in a concrete cell because they wanted me trained? What gall! What was going on? I was kidding myself. I knew what I was being trained for.

I fumed and cursed and threatened any number of fanciful punishments on my captors. I spent hours in my rage. Finally I tired of threatening fanciful reprisals far beyond my ability to achieve. I resigned myself to learning only through osmosis. I could not affect my environment. I couldn't ask questions. All I could do was breathe, eat, sleep, use the pail, and mince to the limit of my tether. I don't think any healthy young woman was ever so helpless. I despaired. I would fight them, but I knew that they had time and the ability to cause me pain. They could condition me to be whoever they wanted. Pain was all it took to change any woman.

I slept curled on my mat. I woke but couldn't bring myself to practice kneeling and standing. That was too depressing to contemplate. Master appeared with a water bottle. I struggled to kneel. He removed my gag and I drank all the water.

He said, "You did not practice kneeling and standing as I told you."

"No, Master," I said, "it was too hard."

He walked behind me and with deft motions squeezed my arms together and wrapped a couple of turns of cord around them, just below my elbows. He put his knee against my back and pulled and pulled on the cords, forcing my arms together. When my elbows touched and my arms were welded together, he tied the cord off. It hurt terribly. My shoulders ached already from the unnatural strain. But the cord itself was worse. He had only used a couple of turns and the thin cord bit into my flesh like a fanged creature.

I sobbed, "Please, Master, that hurts terribly. I can't stand it. Please take it off."

He said, "Practice kneeling and standing. Switch back and forth. You must be graceful and make no unnecessary motions. I'll check later and when you're sufficiently proficient I will feed you. The cord on your elbows is punishment for disobedience." He left.

I was in so much pain I couldn't do anything but cry and try to think of a way to mitigate the pain. After a while the pain decreased to a dull, intense ache. The sharp tang had diminished.  I was hungry so I got back into the kneeling position.  I strained to get my knees far enough apart that I could feel my pussy lips part.  I tried different positions of my feet and legs to let me get my pussy on the ground.  I practiced thrusting my breasts out and staring at the floor. When I thought I was doing OK, I stood.  My motion wasn't graceful .  I had work ahead of me.

I worked on these positions for a long time.  I thought of resting but remembered food.  I kept at it.  Finally, Master reappeared with a food bowl and another water bottle.  I knelt, trying to get everything perfect in one motion.

He said, "You're showing improvement.  Stand."

I stood, managing to get up and in position in one motion.

He said, approvingly, "Good.  Not perfect, but a definite improvement.  Practice these moves and postures  at least twenty times a day. Now kneel and eat." He set the bowl on the ground in front of me.

It was demeaning to eat like an animal, but that's where the food was, I ate it all and licked the bowl.  It was a tasteless porridge with bits of fish and vegetables.  It was delicious. When I sat up, Master wiped some food off my nose ring and chin.

"Master, may I speak? "

"Yes, what is it?"

"I'm sorry I didn't obey you. Would you consider removing the cord on my elbows?"

"Not yet. Disobedience warrants a more severe punishment than a mere slip up. The cord stays on for a while longer. Continue your practices." He left.

I was able to maintain a calm demeanor until he was gone then I broke down sobbing and mouthing my mantra, "It isn't fair. It isn't..." After the tears stopped I started practicing again. It was a way to take my mind off the continual pain. Master removed the cord before lights out. It hurt almost as much as the blood flow resumed. I would be very careful not to disobey in the future.

# Chapter 8 : Shod

In a few days another chained girl was put somewhere close to me. Master talked to her and I heard her call the other girl Rayna. After I heard Master leave I tried talking to the new girl. She didn't answer me and I thought she might be gagged. I remembered a trick I saw on a TV medical show. The patient couldn't talk, so they used a simple code. The doctor would ask a yes/No question and one blink of the eye meant yes, two meant no. I was able to ask a few simple questions but didn't learn anything of value. She was female and a slave, but I needed to think of better questions. We stopped when she indicated she was tired of the 'Talking.'

Master would feed me first, then the other, Rayna. He was always gagged unless Master was with us, so we didn't get to speak for long time.

I had no day or night. Master came irregularly and fed and watered me. My pail was emptied every three or four feedings. My only timepiece was my whippings. They happened every other day, after my first feeding, regular as clockwork. Someone strong would lift me onto my feet, take off my gag, pull me to the end of my tether, and lift my bound wrists high, until I was on tiptoe facing the ring holding me to the wall. I would receive twenty fierce strokes of a whip or cane on my tight ass and the backs of my legs. They came fast and hard. My screams filled the air. After the strokes I was left hanging for a long time.

Then I would hear Rayna whipped. She screamed as loud as me. Then my hands would be released. No words were ever spoken. My whip wielder said nothing and I did not have permission to speak.

I could reach my wounded bottom with my fingers. It was practically all I could reach. I stroked my bottom, tracing the weals and soothing the fire with my touch. I always wondered how long I would be whipped. I knew I was guilty and deserved punishment, but for how long and was this life all. I knew my pain and humiliation would play a continual role in my punishment, but was there an end?

Every day, after the whipping or after feeding, Rayna would be taken somewhere and be returned after several hours. I never learned why.

I rubbed my hands on the welts to sooth them. The punishment never broke the skin, but sitting was a torture only slightly less than the whip itself.

Days passed. I lost count. I had no way to record or recollect anything. I had watched movies and read books involving interrogation. I had been cut off from most environmental clues. It was possible that even likely my diurnal clock was intentionally being confused. All they had to do was vary my feeding times and whipping times. I didn't have any other clues to time of day. My God. I was being conditioned to .. what? I didn't know for sure, but they seemed intent on making me dependent on Master. They weren't interrogating me. I hadn't been asked anything. I was just being punished and conditioned.

I was given shoes. Lady-like shoes. One day after eating, Master had me stand facing the wall and pulled first one foot then the other up behind me and slipped a shoe on me. A strap encircled my ankle and pulled tight and was then locked. When he lowered my feet, I had on at least four inch heels.

If I stood with my feet touching, my hobble chain just touched the floor. If I walked, all I heard was the tinkle of the links shifting. The annoying clatter of my chain dragging on the floor was gone. My stride wasn't affected, but my balance was a little more unsteady. I hadn't worn heels this high very often. They made me change my positioning of my feet a little when I was kneeling. Without shoes I could rest with my toes flexed so their sole was on the ground I could rock backwards to stand. With shoes covering my toes I had to rest the top of the shoe on the ground and rock over the toe to start. It relieved some stress on my toes, but took just an instant longer to stand. Master shod Rayna similarly, from the sounds. I only heard the click of her heels and a tinkle of chain. Master was keeping us similarly equipped.

The only visitor I knew of was Master. I may have had visitors I didn't detect. Cameras may have broadcast my boring plight to millions. I learned to piss and crap adroitly in a pail. Never missed. Never wiped, either. I was able to hold my ass cheeks wide apart with my chained hands as I squatted. Worked OK, but I have acquired an aroma.

One day my routine changed. Master unlocked my chain from the wall and helped me stand. He led me some ways. I passed through several doors. The floor changed from concrete to tile after a while.

My feet were pulled apart and fastened to the floor. I felt my tether fastened above my head. I had to stand tall to avoid choking.

"Its time for a proper whipping Lagina. You may scream or if you wish I will gag you."

"Master, I know you will whip me, but I would like to know if I am being punished. I would like to correct my behavior if so."

"Of course you are being punished. You were to receive twenty. Now you will receive twenty five because of the question." He pulled my chained wrists high on my back and fastened them to my collar.

I do not want the gag, Master."

"All right. I will give you an opportunity. If you do not scream I will retract the last five strokes. It will be a chance for you to excel, Lagina."

"Thank you, Master. I will try." I would try. Removing five strokes was a worthy goal. If I could show obedience under the whip, perhaps he will be more lenient with me later.

Good. Count the strokes and thank me after each one."

"Yes, Master."

The first scalding stroke lashed across my upper back. The pain was bad, but not as bad as I feared. I stifled my scream. I could do this. "One. Thank you, Master."

A long pause then the second stroke landed on my waist and curled around to caress my tummy. Again, it was bad, but I could stand it. I didn't scream. A ladylike whimper escaped me, but that was all. "Two. Thank you, Master."

The third hit the top of my ass cheeks. It was much harder than the first two. I was sure I was bleeding. I felt my flesh recoil under the force. I strained against my bonds to no avail. It was terrible to have to just stand still and take the pain. My helplessness compounded the pain. I longed to be able to rub my wound and soothe it. I clamped my mouth shut and whimpered softly. I held my scream in and realized I felt it more in silence. I was proud of my fortitude. I opened my mouth . "Three. Thank you, Master."

The rest all hit my ass as hard as the third one. I kicked and squealed and stamped my feet. I didn't scream. My poor, poor ass. It would hurt for a week.

"Well done, Lagina. Were you trying to obey or prove something to yourself?"

"Master, I think a little of both."

"Good answer. I'm going to shave you then wash you, Lagina. Don't move."

"Thank you, Master."

The lather felt warm and tingly as he spread it on my pussy. I heard high heels approach and I think a woman took over from Master. It was probably Mistress, but I couldn't tell. Her strokes with the razor were gentle and smooth. I could feel my traitorous body responding to the stimulation. I felt the warmth growing in my loins. I heard a soft moan come floating out of me. I shifted my loins involuntarily.

"Keep still, Lagina."

"Yes, mistress. I didn't move on purpose."

"I know. You're a hot bitch aren't you?"

"No, mistress, I think I'm normal,"

"Maybe that's why you're here."

"But, mistress, I never flirted or played around. I have a husband." That wasn't true. I had several lovers while my husband was ill. I don't think he knew. But I had needs even while he was unable to perform. But I wasn't going to tell her that.

"Don't know, Lagina. Your body is superb. Maybe your new owner thinks you were too cold?"

"Mistress, I belong to you. You are my owner. No man can have me."

A fiery cut  on my already bruised ass made me scream.

"No arguing. You contradicted me, Lagina."

"Yes, mistress, Sorry."

She lathered my body all over. She seemed to pay special attention to my loins and ass. She rinsed me off with a stream of warm water and ran her hands all over my body. It felt so good just to be touched again. She massaged my breasts and squeezed and pinched my nipples until they were rock hard and ached in a good way.

As she lathered me I felt strange movements like weights tugging on my nipples and labia, At first I dismissed them as a result of my long lack of mobility and maybe her cloth. But they kept on. At last I recognized the feeling. It was the same thing I felt with heavy earrings when  I turned my head. My nipples and labia were ringed. Oh God. I was ruined. I was adorned like a low class whore. My belly was spasming. I realized the thought of those erotic rings imposed on my body were making me aroused. So this is how I react to subjugation? Mistress' cupped my breasts and I gasped, "Mistress?" Her fingers rolled my ringed nipples and they caught fire. They got rock hard and ached with need, my squeal at her pinch was involuntary and cut short when a torrent of scalding love juices flooded into my belly and my bottom gyrated in abandon as I spasmed frantically, ringed and helplessly chained, in the terrifyingly intense throes of a massive slave orgasm.

Then I understood I was being intentionally aroused by Mistress. While I had been thinking about my rings, she had been stimulating my body.

My belly was still spasming, throbbing rhythmically when she moved her hands lower and stroked my labia lips until I was panting. Her fingers slipped into my well lubricated cunt, then I felt her tongue thrust into my mouth. Her head leaned to my left. I felt my nose ring pushed to the side. Then I felt her nose ring press into my lip beside mine. It was strangely erotic to know our rings were pressed between our faces. I wished I could see and feel them. They were large and smooth and felt the same. She kissed me hard and long while her busy fingers warmed my belly. I didn't know what to do. The kiss was erotic and felt wonderful. I reached my tongue out and felt the ring hanging down to her upper lip and it was thick. I moaned when she left my mouth and even louder when she stuck her tongue into my pussy. She sucked and licked all over my cunt. I felt her ring sliding over my pussy. It was as erotic as her tongue. When she took my clit into her mouth I exploded into a second fantastic orgasm. I writhed and screamed my pleasure as the flaming cauldron of my belly spasmed hard and I tried to curl into a ball, but my restraints held fast. My belly spasmed and my scalding love juices flooded into my pussy and gushed down my legs.

"Guess I'll have to wash your legs again, won't I, Lagina?"

"Yes, mistress," I gasped, still recovering "sorry, but thank you so much, mistress."

"Lagina, you get to return the favor now."

"Mistress, I would like that. May I ask you a question?"

"No, Lagina. But I will tell you I wear a nose ring. All the women here are ringed. We will wear them always.

"Mistress, do you like it?"

"Lagina, you are getting close to a whippable question so be careful. Yes, I do like the way it looks and feels."

"Mistress, I hope this doesn't earn me a whipping, but I wonder if you ever take it out?"

"Silly girl. I can't take it out. My master put it in me and its permanent. I still love it for the way it looks and for its symbolism. No more questions now."

I felt helpless but I was also ashamed of my instant longing. I was still helpless. I felt her lips on mine. I ran my tongue over her ring. It was huge and solid. I opened my mouth in sudden lust. I kissed her back and our tongues danced in my mouth. I felt my heat rising again. I wanted to love her as she had loved me. I felt a pang of guilt, but it was swiftly disposed of by my heat.

She rubbed her breasts against mine. I discovered her breasts were naked too. I never suspected until now. She had a master so she must be a slave. Was she usually naked or did she just want to keep her clothes dry when she shaved and washed me?

I knelt in slow motion, kissing her flesh all the way down. She was naked. My hungry lips found her labia lips and I licked them, one at a time. When I heard her moans of pleasure, I slipped my tongue between them and licked her inner cunt lips. Her love juice was sweet and musky. I loved it. Her breathing became rapid and gasping. I felt her belly spasming inside. I found her clit and sucked it into my mouth. I sucked and licked it until she came. Her love juices spurted warmly down my breasts. She backed up, out of my reach and said, "Thank you Lagina, you were wonderful. Now it looks like I have to wash us both again."

She lathered me and ran her slippery hands over my breasts. I was so hot I almost cam again.

As she lathered me she said, Lagina, I have to tell you, your tongue ring is fantastic. It set me on fire as soon as you licked me. You're going to be very much in demand among the girls. I wouldn't be surprised if a woman buys you once your tongue becomes well known."

After we were both clean and dry, she freed my ankles and led me back to my cell or room, whatever. I felt so much better, so clean, so alive after my orgasm. For now, at least, I didn't care much about my condition.

My world now was darkness, chains, pain, and Master. Master brought me pain at times. Master and pain was better than no Master, I realized. Without her, my world was empty and lonely. I would play with my chains for want of any other distraction. I would kneel near the wall then stretch my hands down as far as I could. If I made my hobble chain tight, I could reach it with my hands. I would rattle it and pull it up, forcing my feet closer together. I would count the links and feel them for imperfections. I came to know each of my inflexible links as old friends, companions in my plight.

Sometimes they were familiar enemies, agents of my captor. Forcing helplessness upon me. Other times they were just my companions on an endless voyage. It was a voyage of patient discovery for me. I found obedience and subjugation. They weren't as bad as I had feared. I came to like them quite a lot, especially since they brought a friend: freedom from pain. Mistress was correct. The whip did teach me to be respectful and to accept what was. My old life faded and I stopped thinking of freedom. I learned patience. But my need became stronger and filled my idle thoughts. I needed to be fucked, badly.

I heard his familiar footsteps approaching. I knelt with proper posture and said, "Greetings, Master."

"Hello, Lagina."

"Hello Master. I feel you are my only friend here. Would you make love to me?"

He replied, "I thought it was about time. Of course I will fuck you. I am known as a superb lover by all the girls here. Lay back on you mat, pull you feet up to your ass and spread your legs wide."

"Master, I said, "Could you release my arms. I would like to touch you."

"No, Lagina, your performance is better if your arms are under you. It puts your pussy in better alignment for me. Your cuffs are wide and will support your body well. Now get in position."

"Yes, Master." I obeyed his commands and felt his hands running up my legs, past my loins and cup my breasts. I felt a spasm ripple outward from my belly, heating me into arousal.

Oh boy. I was going to get fucked. Hard I hope. He played with my nipple rings. Unnecessary, since my nipples were hard as rock already. I was hot. My submissive mind took over. I would have knelt and kissed his feet if I had more time. I was his helpless prey. His slave girl. I was broken for sure. I knew I was his. I accepted that. I wanted him to take me, and the sooner the better.

He ran his fingertips over my nether lips then held them to my mouth. I licked them clean. I was quite tasty, but I needed seasoning. Maybe a little salt? "Master, please fuck me, hard. please?

I heard him unzip his pants and take his cock out. It rubbed against my thigh and was stiff as a board. A nice round board I wanted in me as soon and as deep as possible.

"Please Master, I need you in me. I beg to be fucked, master."

His knees landed between my spread legs and I felt the tip of his cock nuzzling my pussy lips. He thrust strongly and slipped inside my sopping lips. My pussy spasmed around him. Pulling him deeper. He pumped in and out. The slippery friction of his big penis drove me wild. I thrashed uselessly. My hands and feet were locked together. I couldn't gct any leverage tu muve anything. His weight pressed me into the mat deliciously. I moaned at every thrust, my eyes closed, savoring the pleasure. I came around him in a ferocious spasm. My back arched and lifted him. I was so wonderfully helpless and so tightly controlled. My subjugation thundered through me like a river of fire.

He was still pumping my arousal higher. There was no dimming of the heat, my arousal was being pumped higher. Higher than I had ever gone before. I was like a leaf in a hurricane. I was being taken to a place vastly different than any yet seen. His orgasm sprang forth, filling me with his hot, wonderful seed. My orgasm burst in a responsive firework of stars. I swooned. It was heavenly. I couldn't stand it, yet I did. When I could think again, he was still in me. I loved his feel. I knew he would soon withdraw and I hated the thought.

He stayed in me until he had shrunk to his resting state then he pulled out. He said, "Kneel."

I struggled up and I felt his wet penis touch my chin. He ordered, "Clean me." I opened my mouth and he inserted his penis. I licked and sucked our combined juices until I had them all. He was starting to come alive and raised my hopes when he withdrew again. Damn.

" Stand up."

I struggled up and waited as he unlocked me from the wall.

"Its time for your whipping Lagina. Don't make a fuss or it will be worse."

"I won't, Master. I will obey you if you need to unlock my hands or something. You were right. The whip has taught me obedience."

"Yes, Lagina, you are progressing nicely." She took me only a short distance. Just further into my room, I think.

She had me lay on my back. My ankles were raised into the air and I was lifted until my head left the floor. My feet were pulled as far apart as my hobble allowed. I hung in an inverted 'Y' and my tether was fastened to the floor. A rope tied my wrists to the back of my waist. I felt my breasts hanging the wrong way. It was distressing.

"Lagina, ask me to whip you."

Oh God. What can I do? He will whip me anyway. I don't want to be whipped. I can't stand this much pain. He wants me to ask. I must comply. I survived whippings before. "Master, please whip me as much as I need."

"All right, Lagina. You will only receive ten strokes. I will stripe the insides of your legs and your pussy. I want you to count them and thank me for each one. You may scream. Some girls think it relieves the pain."

The first stroke left a fiery line on the inside of my left thigh. It hurt so bad. It was much worse than on my ass. I screamed in pain. I had wanted to keep it in, but there was no way. I thought I would pass out from it. When me need to cry out passed, I said, "One. Thank you Master."

He paused before the next stroke. When it landed, its pain compounded the residual hurt from the first stroke. It was too much. I lost control. I screamed and twisted around for some time. I regained control and was ashamed of how poorly I behaved. I knew I was beyond control. The pain was too great. He would kill me with ten. I couldn't stand it. "Two. Thank you, Master."

The pain crescendoed for each of the rest. I behaved miserably. My helpless screams and gyrations must have gladdened the heart of everyone watching. I was completely out of control and begging for mercy. I managed to count and thank Master for each one, but only after a lot of commotion. Next time I would ask for a gag.

I received six on my legs. Foolishly I thought I was more than halfway done. The next two landed on my pussy lips, causing them to swell and throb uncontrollably. I knew the next one would kill me. Master had one more surprise for me. Number nine hit the bottoms of my breasts sending such terrible, sharp pains through me I thought I had been stabbed with a knife, I felt the stab of pain all the way to my throbbing pussy as If I had been impaled with a four foot long lance. I squealed and screamed and jerked my collar hard against its tether. I wept for minutes and couldn't stop sobbing.

Master's voice came to me. "Count and thank me or I will start over."

I wailed, "Nine, thank you, Master," and the unbearable pain came again to my breasts. I fainted.

I was still hanging from my ankles when I regained consciousness, Every part of me hurt. I was always left alone for a long time after I was punished. This was no different. Slave girls learn to have patience. I hurt. I felt like I had been cut to ribbons. I expected I was bleeding heavily from my tattered skin. I didn't feel any liquid running down my legs but they hurt like blazes. The wonder was that I survived. I thought I would die because I couldn't stand it. But I did stand it. I was unable to avoid the pain so I had to endure it. It was not pleasant, but I did endure it and I still lived.

I finally had a companion so I didn't have to fondle my chain. I had pain. I found that I could twist my body around and increase my pain. The pain was lessened if I stayed still. I played with my pain like I used to scratch scabs until they bled. I had nothing else to do. Eventually Master returned.

He said, "Lagina, think about what happened here. Tell me what you learned."

"Master, I learned that I can endure pain and still live. Am I bleeding much?"

"I will forgive you that question. Silly girl. You are not bleeding at all. You only have some pretty red stripes on your legs and breasts." He took me down and removed the rope from my wrists. He pulled my wrists high on my back and locked them to the chain, close to my collar. Then He locked the end of the chain somewhere over my head.

# Chapter 9 : Training Rayna

[Manuel and Katy agreed it was important for Rayna's initial training to be under a woman.]

The woman entered my cell and said, "Rayna, kneel whenever you see me or a master."

I said, "I am a Prince. I kneel only to my King."

She smiled and without a word started hitting me with her whip. I fell and twisted every way I could. I tried to run but my chains held me fast. I said I was sorry. I begged her to stop. I realized at last that only by kneeling would she stop. I struggled into a kneeling position, sobbing with the pain, my back bowed to protect my face and sensitive breasts.

She stopped hitting me and said, "You're inappropriately arrogant for a chained slave girl. Do you understand your new status, Rayna?"

I sobbed and choked out, "Mistress, yes, I do, but ingrained feelings and pride die reluctantly."

"You will be punished for the slightest imperfection. You must learn to kneel proudly. Straighten up. Arch your back and thrust your breasts out. Spread your legs wide. I want to see inside your cunt."

I tried to comply. My body hurt all over from her whip. "Yes, Mistress."

She corrected me, "Wider. Hold your head high and keep your eyes on the floor. Never look a Mistress or Master in the eye. Get your cunt as close to the floor as possible. In the future you will be expected to put your cunt on the floor. You may only kneel or stand in here. You can sleep laying down. You will not speak without permission unless acknowledging an order or responding to a question or order. You will address me as Mistress. Do you understand your rules?"

"Yes, Mistress." I really did. I would do my best to obey. The whip is a great teacher.

"Good. Stand up."

I stood as quickly as I could, but I was hampered by my chains.

"Stop. Kneel again."

I sank back down.

"Put your feet as far apart as you can. Make you hobble taut. Put your toes flat on the floor. Rock back on your heels so you are squatting, then extend your legs. Do it."

I did as ordered and it was much better than trying one foot as a time as I had earlier.

"Now, just like when kneeling, arch your back, thrust your breasts out, hold your head high and keep your eyes on the floor."

I shifted as ordered.

She said, "Good, Rayna. Now let's practice these two positions. Kneel. Stand...."

She had me switch back and forth ten times. I guess I did OK because I didn't earn any more strokes of the whip.

When I was standing she said, "Stop. Stay standing."

I obeyed.

"Now I'm going to add a command. When you hear, 'Leash,' you will tilt your head back and look at the ceiling. At the same time, stick your tongue out. Hold this position until told to relax. This will make it easier for me or a master to put your leash on any of your rings. Your nipple, nose, and cunt rings are easily accessible all the time. This makes your collar and tongue rings also accessible. Clear?"

"Yes, Mistress." It was clear and abhorrent, but it was obey or be whipped. I was ashamed of how easily I was subjugated by a little pain. But what choice did I have. I was helpless. I knew I was being conditioned to obedience. Shit.

She held up a chain leash and said, "Leash."

I tilted my head back and stuck out my tongue.

She clipped a leash on my nose ring and said, "Relax." She unlocked the chain from the back of my collar.

"Rayna, proper heeling procedure is you walk one pace to my left and one pace behind me. You keep your eyes on me and track my movements. I should never feel a tug on your leash. If I feel too many or too strong a tug, you will be punished. If I stop, kneel beside me. Clear?"

"Yes, Mistress." I was terrified. Was she going to walk me in public? Show me off. Humiliate me in front of strangers? If I didn't obey I'd be whipped for sure. I knew I couldn't resist the leash's pull on my nose ring. I would be the obedient little slave girl they wanted. Shit.

"Heel." She turned and walked out of the cell. I hurried to get in position. I had felt only the briefest of tugs and it made me sure I didn't want it to happen again. I kept my head erect and straight ahead. I kept my eyes on my Mistress. I wanted nothing now except to hell well.

She led me out of the corridor of cells and into a larger room. There were maybe twenty slave girls in the room milling

110

about. A break from training, maybe. Mistress led me to the center of the room and stopped. I knelt on her left side, and adjusted my posture.

She said, loudly, "Girls, this is Rayna. She's new. She used to be male before she made the wrong people angry. She doesn't know anything about being a girl, so I'm going to teach her the rudiments. He was an arrogant male who had no respect for women. If you get the chance, show her what males expect from a lowly slave girl. My instructions are to see that Rayna and Lagina, a natural female who was his accomplice, both are humiliated forever. I would appreciate any suggestions for their training or anything else."

The slaves all gathered around me. A redhead said, "Once a male, huh. The Doctors did a good job. She looks like a girl. I bet her head is still full of male shit. We can help there, Mistress."

I tried not to let my fear show on my face. It took every ounce of willpower to keep my face calm. All the girls looked angry. Even though their ankles were chained, their hands were free and I could a the joy they felt at having a former male at their mercy. One of the males who kept them down, treated them as something less than men, and who now enslaved them. I didn't want to be at their mercy. I don't think it mattered much to them that I was now a slave girl too.

Mistress said, "Not now girls. I need to do some more training first. She and Lagina will be available to you soon.

She started walking again and I leapt up, not only to keep my leash slack, but anxious to leave the pack of slave girls who looked at me so wolfishly. She led me through a locked door and into a , a, well, a makeup room. There was a long counter with six small sinks, backed by a continuous mirrored wall. There were short stools close to the sinks and in front of each stool were arrayed brushes and tweezers and a host of cosmetics. A length of chain was bolted to the counter in front of each stool. She led me to a stool and ordered, "Kneel on the stool and raise as high as you can."

I obeyed. She locked the short chain to my collar and unlocked my wrists.

"Stretch your arms. Limber them up."

I obeyed.

After I had stretched for a while she said, "Pay attention." She then pointed to each cosmetic and named it and described its use. She did the same for each brush, pencil and tweezer. She had e apply a red lipstick then critiqued my action. She had me remove it and reapply it. When I had performed to her satisfaction she taught me mascara, rouge, eye shadow. eye liner, eyebrow shaping and pencil. Next was a scarlet paint on my nipples and cunt lips. I learned to paint my finger and toenails.

She let me stop after I had applied all the cosmetics on the counter. I had to admit I looked the part of a pleasure slave.

She locked my hands behind me and released my collar from the counter. She strapped high heels shoes on my feet and said, ""Now you'll learn to walk like a lady. Stand up."

I stood and adjusted my posture as she required. I was unsteady on the heels. She said, OK, to walk in heels, have the heel make contact first then rock forward on the heel. At each step, place your foot exactly in front of the rear foot. I'll hold your arm to steady you. Walk evenly and slowly. Go,"

She took hold of my arm and helped me walk. Her instructions seemed to work. I walked steadily and I could see it would only take a little practice to become proficient. I walked up and down the length of the room several times. She released my arm and said, "Go on."

She led me by the leash and we went back and forth many times. She varied my speed from a slow walk to a rush. In the end I didn't receive any more whip blows, so I guess I did all right. I practiced kneeling and standing in heels and learned it was almost the same as barefoot.

She said, "You learn quickly, that's good."

"Thank you, Mistress."

She said, "When I take you back to your cell, I will take off Lagina's hood and leave your gag off. I'm sure you've identified her as the former Queen Lorraine. This afternoon tell Lagina you once were Ramalah."

"Mistress, may I speak?"

"Yes."

"Mistress, I don't wish Lagina to know I was once her lover. Whether she feels contempt or pity for me it will be terribly humiliating."

"Rayna, the King wants you humiliated and humble. Tell her or I will whip you and tell her myself."

"Yes, Mistress," I said dispiritedly.

She took me back to my cell and locked the tether chain to the back of my collar. I knelt as required and watched as she went across the passage and talked to a kneeling Lagina for a moment then removed her hood. Mistress left and I watched as Lagina slowly opened her eyes and adjusted to the dim lighting. I said, "Hello, I'm Rayna. You're Lagina?"

Lagina looked at me and asked, "You look familiar. Have we met before?"

No point in delaying it. I wonder how she'll react? Disbelief? Joy? Derision? Humor? Pity? Sympathy? Anger? I wouldn't blame her for any or all emotions. It was truly my fault she was here and no longer Queen. Stupid woman. I would lead her to the answer. I smiled and said "Our mistress made me practice applying makeup. Do you like it?"

"It looks good. Why did you have to practice?"

"I had never used it before. I had to learn from scratch."

She stared at me. "You're beautiful. How is it that you never used makeup before?

I replied, "I've only looked like this for a few days. I didn't need it before."

"A few days? What happened?"

"Plastic surgery. I didn't feel a thing. I didn't ask for it either."

"You mean someone operated on you without your permission? Were you deformed before?"

"No. I was male before the operation. You knew me. Quite well."

She stared at me. "Rama?"

"Hello Lorraine," I said."

She just stared at me for a long time. Finally, she laughed, "Hah-Hah-Hah,  Boy you really got what you deserved, didn't you.  I guess the King wanted to keep you around but make sure you couldn't lust after his job again, huh?"

"Yes," I agreed. I can't ever get his job.  I think his real goal was to  make me live in humiliation.  You too.  Now he can screw us whenever he wants, show us off to everyone as examples of what can happen if they misbehave, and be merciful that by letting us live.  How are you coping?"

"OK. My life in chains is alternatively painful, arousing, and boring.  We will have to learn to be patient.  We can only wait in our cells until someone takes us out to do something or be punished.  They don't let you make any decisions."

"Yeah," I agreed, "I met some other slave girls when I was taken out this morning.  Their hands wore cuffs like ours but were not restrained.  Have you heard how this place works?  Can we expect to have our hands released if we follow the rules?

"I don't know, Lagina said, "but I doubt it  I thing they are just being trained and will be sold.  We're here to be punished and trained.  I think we'll be sent back to Jedrah when they're done with us here."

"Lagina, what do you think about me?"

"You were a good lover. You also blackmailed me into poisoning the King. You were not a nice man, but probably only a little worse than the average male. You were overbearing and domineering. I never had a chance. I loved you and you took advantage of me. I would still be a Queen save for you. I'm angry with Rama. But you're no longer Rama. Now you'll see for yourself how men treat women. I'm happy you're a girl. It seems a fitting punishment. Maybe you'll be a better woman than you were a man."

I replied, "I don't blame you. I don't expect I will have a chance to be anything other than an obedient slave girl now. I think the King will keep us together. I'd like to be your friend now. If I can help you somehow, I will."

"Thank you Rayna. I regret my actions. I was full of indignation and anger with my brother, and I was greedy. I never should have brought you into my plans. I have earned my punishment, though I think my brother is more inventive than I ever thought. He has outdone himself with my punishment. I hope you'll be a friend now. I agree, it looks like we're in this together."

"Rayna," she said, "being a woman isn't that bad. Half the people on the planet are women."

"Lagina, it isn't so much being a woman, its being changed to a woman after thirty years of being a man. All my gestures, my speech, my capabilities, my expectations have been thrown out the window. I have no idea how to behave and I

117

am always comparing myself to what I was. Its the change that's so unsettling."

She replied, Well, From my point of view, being enslaved is just as bad. We have had all or freedoms stripped away. We can't decide where to go, what to do, what to say, what to eat, anything. Everything is under our keeper's control. Isn't that part of your discomfort?"

"Of course," I said, "but they took my manhood. You don't know what that means to a man."

"Yeah, but they gave you a cunt, and that's pretty important to girls, you know. Can you have children?"

"No, thank God. I don't feel the least bit nurturing."


Mistress went into Lagina's cell, put a nose leash on her, unlocked her tether from her collar and led her into my cell. She locked Lagina's leash onto the back of my collar, and unlocked my tether from my collar She led us out of the cell and down the passage to the big room. Someone took Lagina's leash off my collar.

# Chapter 10 : Routines

Rayna and I were always blindfolded when men fucked us. We trained to pleasure and arouse men in many other ways and were allowed to see them. But we never knew who fucked us. Sometimes we were blindfolded when we were whipped. Maybe our masters whipped us too?

The whip or strap or paddle were used to give us pain. If the pain was not too bad, we orgasmed to it. A little pain always shifted to be a lot of pleasure. But when applied hard, pleasure didn't come quickly. A skillful whip handler could give us a lot of pain and then shift it into a stupendous orgasm or two.

Every week we received a hard whipping. Its sole purpose was to remind us we were slaves and restore our fear of our masters. For these whippings there was a special room where we were hung from our wrists, feet off the floor. The whip would leave scarlet stripes all over us. Especially our breasts. We would be hung and left to ponder our fates for an hour or so before the beatings. After the beatings were done, we would hang another hour. They used a whip that didn't cut the skin but left wonderfully colorful stripes. It hurt a lot but never did any damage. We were never gagged for the beatings. I think they liked to hear us beg.

The training manual was quite specific. Slaves in training had to receive a hard whipping every week. Without this the slave would become difficult and require excessive punishment in the future. The recommendation was that her back, thighs, buttocks, stomach. and breasts be a uniform pink all over. The strokes should be no more than five seconds apart. If she had an orgasm, let her hang for an hour and start over. A gag was recommended since a satisfactory punishment was judged by her skin not by her pleas.

The whippings were quite effective in reminding us of our slavery. We were completely broken afterwards. Not that we were ever a problem. It was that just after so many orgasms we tended to get a little sloppy in our speech and posture. This restored us to the straight and narrow paths our trainers and masters desired.

My chains were a constant. My feet were linked by the same short chain all the time. My collar was how I was secured. Whenever I was not escorted by a trainer, I was locked to something solid by my collar. When a trainer was around, they used my light leash to lead me and hold me in place if they were somewhere else in the room. My hands stayed fastened high on my back when I slept and when I didn't need to use my hands. Even if the lock was removed from my hands, I could only move them just in front of my body. The permanent chains to my wrists were fastened to the back of my waist band. Sometimes during the day Master would just lock my hands to the back of my waist band directly. I was pretty helpless wherever he put the lock. The chains were probably of some benefit to me. If I wasn't hopelessly chained, I would be consumed with trying to find a way to escape. That thought never crossed my mind, even when I was still smarting from a beating.

We were kept in complete ignorance of the outside world. We were forced to focus on our training by the simple expedient of not letting us know anything else. No outside news or reading material was ever provided. We were told curiosity was unbecoming for slave girls. Master never told Rayna or I anything in advance. They just gave orders. I learned to live in the present. I learned never to think about anything outside of what I could see or feel. There was no other place than where I was. I felt no anticipation, no expectation. I lived in the instant, for I did not know of anything else and could not affect anything else.

Although I never knew which men had me, we trained with several men quite a lot. Rayna and I had to learn how to please both men and women in other ways than just spreading our legs. There was a lot of skill involved in being a good courtesan.

The trainer's whips were simple braided leather cords with short handles. Never breaking the skin, but always leaving thin red lines wherever they landed. Wielded lightly they corrected my actions and warmed my skin. It leached through to my core and excited me. It made me want more and brought me to the threshold of ecstasy, but they never pushed me over the edge. I loved the feeling and hated the denial. Firmly swung, the same whip scalded me, punished me, controlled me.

After several weeks of training, one light stroke was all it took bring me to the edge. I was not able to orgasm without some direct stimulation of my loins. It took but a single finger to push me over the edge from arousal to a thunderous orgasm. Once I had orgasmed, any further stimulation would send me over again. Any stimulation, whether sex related or pain inducing would send me over the edge again. If my trainer aroused me but did not let me come, I would remain in needy anguish for hours. Until either I finally cooled down or allowed to orgasm. Then it would start all over again.

After I had orgasmed the first time, my later orgasms grew in strength. After five or so I would faint. I had learned to be a slut powerhouse. Once aroused, I would orgasm at almost any touch. My trainer chose whether I orgasmed or was denied release. In my heart I knew I was a true slave. This was where I belonged. My feelings and desires were no longer under my control. Now, I longed for the whip and orgasm. My body could no longer tell the difference between pain and pleasure. Rather, I welcomed pain because it could lead to more pleasure than I had ever known . I knew I could never be free again. I was only and forever a sex slave, and loved it. Even if released tomorrow I would search forever for a man or woman to enslave me again. My desires, my feelings, my preferences no longer mattered. I longed for my master to take me to the heights of pleasure only he could give.

# Chapter 11 : Exercise

Mistress led us up to the front of the room and handed our leashes to a slave she called Tasha. Tasha was the head girl here. I think our Mistress was not part of the chain of command. She and Tasha spoke as equals. We were going to be a part of the daily exercise routine from what she said. The rest of the time we were being punished and trained separately. Tasha called Mistress 'Katy.' Now we knew Mistress' name. Mistress wore the same collar and rings as all the girls but had no other restraints. Tasha had an ankle hobble like everyone else, but nothing on her wrists. Mistress left the room.

Tasha and six men released us, unlocked our hands. Which meant they were still fasted to the back of our belts and we could only reach them about foot in front of us. They formed us up in four rows in the center of the room. Tasha stood in front of us and said, "Position training. New girls do what the others do. Memorize these positions and their names or numbers. Practice them in your cells. Position one, Standing Display." She spread her legs and threw her hands behind her.

I watched and followed Tasha and watched the girls around me for confirmation. Spread my feet as far as my hobble allowed. Wrists crossed behind me. Arch my back and thrust out my breasts. Hold my head high. Aim my eyes to look at the ground. I knew this one. It was like the kneeling position Aaron had taught me except for the standing bit. I was surprised when I felt the sharp sting of an instructors whip on my ass. He said, "Your chain is touching the floor. Tighter."

I ratcheted my feet farther apart until my chain was tight.

I wasn't the only one to be corrected. After the room stilled, Tasha yelled, "I am a slave girl."

The girls around me yelled back, "I am a slave girl." I get it. This was their mantra, their affirmation of their duty. I was sure if I didn't follow, I'd be whipped.

Tasha yelled, "I exist to serve my Master."

Along with the others I yelled, "I exist to serve my Master."

The litany continued. "I am only a female." "I love my chains." "My duty is obedience." "My master's pleasure is my goal." "I love being a girl." "I love being a slave."

It knew it was over when Tasha said, "Position two, Leash."

I watched the girls around me. I had to turn my head half left and tilt it back. Everything else stayed where it was. No stripe this time.

There were twenty four positions that took us onto our knees, front, back, and side as well as standing. I collected ten more stripes, not for doing the positions wrong. But for not gracefully changing positions. It seems we have to be poised and graceful despite our hardware. That's not fair, but nothing about this situation was fair. We had to learn what our masters wanted. It actually excited me to be so obedient.

Finally we finished the positions. Tasha said, "Position One, Standing Display."

I snapped into it easily It was maybe the tenth time this morning I had assumed this position.

Tasha yelled, "What are you?"

Without thinking I yelled back, in unison with the girls around me, "I am a slave girl." I was proud to have known the answer and also dismayed. I was already thinking like a slave.

Tasha yelled, "What is your duty?

"Obedience," I yelled. The litany continued in reverse. We all knew the answers.

"What is your goal?" "My Master's pleasure."

"Do you love your chains?" "I love my chains."

"Do you love being a slave girl?" "I love being a slave girl."

"Why do you exist?" "To serve my Master."

I expected a break, but no. Tasha went right into an exercise program. We stretched then lay on the floor and did core strengthening. Then abs, then we high stepped around the room. Tasha was in great shape. We had to lift our knees as high as our waist as we walked. She kept us walking around the room, all clanking in our ankle chains for a quarter hour. The men had a much easier time trotting beside us, free of any restraints. They used their whips freely. After we had all steadied down and were doing well, Tasha sped up. Now we were jogging with high steps and our chains seldom touched the floor. If your chain touched the floor, it made a clank and you got a stripe. I learned just how good an instructional device the whip was.

When we started flagging, Tasha slowed us back to a walk and we finished up that way. We cooled down and were allowed to shower, ten girls at a time. I was so glad to get the stink off me.

We were fed once a day after our exercises. After our shower our hands were locked high on our backs and we were lined up into four rows. I noticed one row was short two girls. When all the girls were lined up, Tasha barked, "Position three, Kneeling Display."

We all dropped to our knees and assumed the position.

The two missing girls came through a side door, both pushing a silver serving cart. They went down the rows and put a bowl of water and a bowl of food in front of each girl.

When it was delivered they put the remaining bowls in front of their positions and knelt.

Tasha said, "Eat." All the girls bent forward and either lapped up some water or started eating. I heard clanks as their collar rings hit the edge of the metal bowls.

I looked at the bowl in astonishment. Women don't eat out of a bowl on the floor. We're not animals. I don't care if we are slaves, we are still people! I was angry and terrified. I wanted to rebel. Would they punish me if I didn't eat? Did I want to the feel the whip again? Did I just want reassurance of my status? Or did I just want to be aroused by the whip?

A man came up behind me and asked, "Do you need some help?"

I said in a soft voice, "Yes, Master."

A stinging blow landed on my shoulder. He said, " Eat it all now!"

The pain was terrible. My whole body quivered. My shoulders were on fire and my chains held me fast. I realized I had been foolish and resolved to be obedient in the future. Slaves were not permitted dignity or allowed any independent action. "Yes, Master!" I exclaimed, ashamed of both my submission and the sexual heat that had erupted in my belly. I felt like I would climax if he struck me one more time. I hoped he would touch me some other way.

The men watched while we ate. I ate everything in my bowl, a tasteless porridge with bits of meat and vegetable. There was no way to keep my nose ring out of the food, so I got some of the food on my nose ring and my cheeks. I licked the bowl clean when I finished. The same two girls took the bowls and wiped our faces with a damp cloth.

After eating we were allowed free time in the big room. Talking and eating out each other was the only entertainment. I made it my plan to talk to every girl in the facility and learn their stories. After an hour we were ordered to go back to our cells. We could lock ourselves to the chain or Tasha would do it when she made her rounds. When she came in she locked the chain to my collar then she showed me the box of pink pills. Take one a day unless you want a baby. If you forget, tell me. If you get pregnant there will be much punishment. Your master might let you have the child. If its a girl, she'll be a slave here. If a boy, he'll go up for adoption. She left me with my hands locked in position two.

Usually Master, but sometimes Mistress, would come and take us out of our cells for punishment and our special training.

# Chapter 12 : Pleasure

In the big room Katy handed Lagina's leash to Tasha who led her off a few yards, followed by half the girls. Katy kept hold of Rayna's leash, surrounded by the rest of the girls.

Lagina

Mistress gave my leash to someone else. Rayna was unlocked from my collar and taken away. My nose was lifted until I was on tiptoes. I couldn't move and I felt another person unlock my wrists. I didn't even think about escape. The grip on my leash was like iron and my ankles were chained. My hands were lifted and fastened to a bar above my shoulders. The bar was raised until my weight was supported by my wrists. My leash was removed. My feet were off the floor and I swayed gently. My wrists and arms ached from the unaccustomed strain. It wasn't too bad, so I didn't protest. A gag was slipped into my mouth. I had learned it was futile and painful to resist the gag.

The first lash landed on my ass. It was like a bright line of fire. The pain radiated through my ass from that line and twisted my belly. I squealed and kicked my feet trying to lessen the pain. It slowly faded to a dull ache. I received three on my ass. Spaced them out so each had faded a little before the next one hit. I made a lot of noise and used my legs a lot. I swung in a circle and kicked as far as my hobble allowed. I moaned continuously. I felt the heat building in me almost like arousal, but different.

Gentle fingers penetrated my pussy lips and stroked my inner lips. Another pair of hands rubbed my tender ass at the same time. They were arousing me. Or maybe changing my pain to arousal. Now it seemed they weren't so different. Large fingers penetrated me as the hand slipped from my ass onto my breasts. He cupped and stimulated my breasts with one hand as his other hand aroused my loins. Soon I was gasping and squealing with pleasure until I screamed my orgasm into the gag. I had orgasmed from a whipping and fondling. Orgasmed. How weird was that?

He gave me a minute before he resumed my whipping. I received four strokes on the backs of my thighs. They hurt, but it was different now. The pain flashed directly into my belly and stoked my inner fire. I was so hot. I felt his hands on me again and I think he barely touched my pussy lips before I came again. I flooded my pussy with my love juices. He walked around me and rubbed some of my juice into my nostrils. It was a sexy touch and I appreciated his gesture.

He laid three more stripes on the front of my thighs, pausing between strokes. I hardly felt the pain of the lashes. My mind felt the arousal rising in belly much more strongly. At this moment I realized I loved being whipped. It was a perfect way to tame a girl. It was demeaning. It taught her she was helpless before male strength. It showed me that pain was a route to bliss and made me want more. I wanted nothing more than more strokes. It made it clear to me I had been mastered. Master walked to my head and removed my gag. I was gasping and moaning, wanting another release of the cruel heat in my belly.

I heard his command, "Service me, slave."

I knew about oral sex. I hadn't done it, but I knew men liked it. Would I do it to avoid pain. Of course. It didn't change anything and I would be whipped until I did it anyway. I said, "Yes, Master."

The bar lowered and I sank onto my knees. I spread my legs wide and opened my mouth.

I licked the head of his cock and sucked it into my mouth. I licked it more and sucked more of him in. Soon, I had his whole length in my mouth and was pumping like a locomotive. I felt my tongue ring pressing my tongue down and I knew he must be feeling it too. I hope he liked it. He swelled larger until I was afraid he would choke me. I heard him grunting as I got him close to the edge. Then he exploded in me, filling my throat with his hot spend. I swallowed frantically, trying to keep it all in me. I succeeded.

Sucking a man's cock to climax is the greatest act of sexual submission a female can make. I was truly a slave girl now.

I was kneeling, awaiting orders, when a woman put her arms around me and kissed me. Her kiss was hard and delightful. Then, to my surprise more hands touched me. They caressed my ass and fondled my sore breasts. Someone started stroking my pussy and it didn't hurt at all. It felt like several women were caressing me.

I heard soft clattering of chains as women gathered around me. I felt a pussy shoved into my face and heard, "Lick me, suck me, girl."

I leaned closer between and pressed my lips to her labia lips. I licked and sucked on my her engorged skin. My tongue snaked between the labia lips to caress her innermost recesses. I could hear her breathing become quick and shallow and I thought she was getting close to orgasm. I sped up my tongue action. Finally, she grabbed the back of my head. She pulled it into her groin hard and shouting "Now, I'm coming." And come she did. It was an enormous orgasm. The churning convulsions rumbled on and on for what seemed like hours. I could hear the smile in her voice when she said, "That was amazing. Your tongue ring was wonderful."

My face was wet with her love juices. I said," Thank you, Mistress."

I heard another girl say, "My turn." She backed away and was quickly replaced by another. I gave eleven slave girls

132

great orgasms by the time they stopped. All of them praised my tongue stud for making me "The Best."

The bar was raised, standing me up. I was immediately caressed by many hands. I couldn't even tell how many there were. They shifted continually. it was like I was surrounded by women who were rubbing every part of me. I felt fingers kneading by breasts and tweaking my rings, rubbing my weals and my pussy and my ears and my belly, every part of me. I felt arousal spreading through me. Soon I was gasping and pleading with them to do it harder, faster, deeper. They caressed my breasts, whipped my bottom, played with my rock hard nipples, then punished my thighs, over and over. I screamed and pleaded for mercy then moaned in unbearable pleasure as my belly jumped and trembled with scalding heat and love juices poured in to my sex as I came again and again in uncountable, endlessly repeating orgasms causing rivulets of love juice down my legs. I slumped and hung from my wrists until someone lifted me. "Don't stop, mistresses, Please."

They didn't stop. The hands moved around. Someone else started kissing me. I had uncounted wonderful orgasms before they stopped. No one said a word the whole time.

Someone released my chain from above. Several sets of hands walked me across the room until my hips were stopped by a horizontal wooden bar. My feet were tied down and I was bent forward over the bar until I was horizontal.

My chain was fastened in front of me, holding me trapped against the bar.

I was helplessly aroused. I couldn't have walked if released. I moaned and writhed in my chains. My loins burned. I was ready to be taken. I was so hot. I needed to climax again. I was needy. I realized I wanted a man in me. I needed to be fucked, hard. My pussy was sopping. I could feel my love juices running down my leg. I moaned and it turned into a scream of pleasure as fingers stroked my pussy. I screamed and pleaded to be fucked over and over. Suddenly a huge cock plunged into my sopping cunt. It was a fitting climax to a surprising and increasingly wonderful set of events. I was taken to heaven with two strokes of this cock. I climaxed again and again as he pumped me up. Finally, I felt him come in me. His hot seed flowed into me like a geyser. I instantly climaxed my final time. It was overwhelming. It was glorious. I lay across the bar, contented and empty. I was content to be a slave. I had never felt this good when free.

Someone freed my chain and I raised up. My feet were untied and I was led to the bath. I really needed cleaning.

"Lagina, did you enjoy yourself?"

"Yes, Mistress. I loved every minute of it, at least after the whipping. It was a really good way to recover."

She cleaned me up and took me back to a cell. I didn't mind being there this time. I just wanted to sleep and lay on my mat. I realized I was in Rayna's cell from the extra mat on the floor and the other chain hanging from a ring in the wall. Then she did something new. After she fastened the tether to the back of my collar, she released my wrists and pulled them up high on my back and locked them to the tether chain. A reverse prayer position.

I asked, "Mistress..."

She said, "This is now how I will fasten your hands when they aren't required. Every time I do this, I will pull them as high as I can. Over time, your tendons will stretch until I can lock your wrists to your collar. In a little while you will adapt to it."

It was painful and more restrictive than before. It would be harder to use the waste pail, for one thing. It sure wasn't needed for security. I was already chained so I couldn't run, chained to a wall, and locked in a barred cell. Just another punishment I guess. At least it wasn't as bad as when she tired my elbows together. Small favors.

I was too tired to care and dropped off immediately.

## Rayna

Mistress led me away from Lagina. We didn't go far. Someone strong, a big man I think took hold of my leash with his huge hand touching my nose. He lifted my nose until I was on tiptoes. A gag was stuffed in my mouth. I had learned. When a gag was put to my lips, I opened my mouth. Resistance was painful and futile.

I couldn't move and I felt another person unlock my wrists. I didn't even think about escape. The grip on my leash was like iron and my ankles were chained. My hands were lifted and fastened to a bar so they were above my shoulders. The bar was raised until my weight was supported by my wrists. He took my leash off. My feet were off the floor and I swayed gently. My wrists and arms ached from the unaccustomed strain. I begged, "Please let my feet reach the floor."

I felt a line of red hot pain form across my breasts. I yelped and felt hot tears wet my blindfold. A man said, You did not receive permission to speak."

The first lash landed on my ass. It was like a bright line of fire. The pain radiated through my ass from that line and twisted my belly. I squealed and kicked my feet trying to lessen the pain. It slowly faded to a dull ache. I received three on my ass. Spaced them out so each had faded a little before the next one hit. I made a lot of noise and used my legs a lot. I swung in a circle and kicked as far as my hobble allowed. I moaned continuously, it seemed. I felt the heat building in me almost like arousal, but different.

Hanging from her chained wrists, aroused beyond bearing, and punished by her Master, the whipsawed brunette could not hold back her enforced submission as her Master's fingers and whip mercilessly imposed delicious torment on her. He caressed her breasts, whipped her bottom, played with her rock hard nipples, then punished her thighs, over and over. She screamed and pleaded for mercy then moaned in unbearable pleasure as her belly jumped and trembled with scalding heat and love juices poured in to her sex as she came again and again in uncountable, endlessly repeating orgasms.

Pain and pleasure mixed into an indistinguishable frenzy of passion and Rayna did not know whether she begged for mercy or more of the ruthless subjugation that filled her with fantastic excitement and lust. It really didn't matter what she wanted, for her Master was not going to heed her pleas. His goal was neither immediate nor urgent.

The cauldron of slave heat in her belly merged with the sting of her whip striped skin to send her dazed mind into a maelstrom of complete and willing submission. Her screams of pain and helplessness shrank into soft moans of lust and need. There was no resistance or free will left in her. She wanted nothing more than to be his complete and total slavegirl. She accepted his complete dominance over her and would obey every order, seek every opportunity to serve him and savor the delight of pleasuring him. The opinions and words of others were no longer relevant. She was going to live blissfully in subspace forevermore. All she wanted now was for her Master to take her, to fill her love canal with his hot member. Then she would be complete.

He left me hanging there, writhing in my chains, helpless and unable to stop my unceasing spasms. Finally I slowed and hung limp from my wrists. Glad I could wind down from my frantic mania of passion. The dull ache of my wrists was my only companion for a long, long time. I had begun to feel normal when he returned.

His questing fingers were a surprise, stroking my labia lips and rubbing my tender ass at the same time. My virgin pussy seemed more sensitive than my penis had been. Maybe it was the hormones. He was arousing me. Or maybe changing my pain to arousal. Now it seemed they weren't so different. His fingers penetrated me as he slipped the hand from my ass onto my breasts. He cupped and fondled my breasts with one hand as his other hand aroused my loins. My nipples were aching and hot. Soon I was gasping and squealing with pleasure until I screamed my orgasm into the gag. I had orgasmed from a whipping and fondling. Orgasmed. How weird was that?

He gave me a minute before he resumed my whipping. I received four strokes on the backs of my thighs. They hurt, but it was different now. The pain flashed directly into my belly and stoked my inner fire. I was so hot. I felt his hands on me again and I think he barely touched my pussy lips before I came again. I flooded my pussy with my love juices. He walked around me and rubbed some of my juice into my nostrils. It was a sexy touch and I appreciated his gesture. When I was a man I thought love secretions were gross. Not so much now.

He laid three more stripes on the front of my thighs, pausing between strokes. I hardly felt the pain of the lashes. My mind felt the arousal rising in belly much more strongly. I had heard of pain sluts. Was I one? Was it his skill? Was it my helpless state, my bondage, forcing my mind to cope with what it couldn't change? Because I was new to this female libido? Master walked to my head and removed my gag. I was gasping and moaning, wanting another release of the cruel heat in my belly.

He bared his rigid cock and said, "Service me, Rayna."

I was shocked and started to protest when I remembered what had happened to me and where I was. I hadn't thought about it before his cock appeared. I had ordered women to use their mouth on my penis when I was male. It was the most erotic event I could remember. To have a woman on her knees before me using her mouth to service me. She was diminished into insignificance while raising me to new heights. It was the ultimate subjugation of woman by man, and I was, externally, at least, a woman. Would I do it to avoid pain. Hell yes. I would be whipped until I did it anyway. I was already the lowest of the low. I said, "Yes, Master."

The bar lowered and I sank onto my knees. I spread my legs wide and opened my mouth.

I licked the head of his cock and sucked it into my mouth. I licked it more and sucked more of him in. Soon, I had his whole length in my mouth and was pumping like a locomotive. I felt my tongue stud and rig pressing into me and I knew it must be stimulating him too. I hope he liked it. He swelled larger until I was afraid he would choke me. I heard him grunting as I got him close to the edge. Then he exploded in me, filling my throat with his hot spend. I swallowed frantically, trying to keep it all in me. I succeeded.

Sucking a man's cock to climax is the greatest act of sexual submission a female can make. I was a slave girl now, no matter how I had begun life.

I was kneeling, awaiting orders, when a woman put her arms around me and pulled me close. Her breasts were bare and ringed. Her kiss was hard and delightful. Then, to my surprise more hands touched me. They caressed my ass and fondled my sore breasts. Someone started stroking my pussy and it didn't hurt at all. It felt like three or four people, women from their soft touch, were caressing me.

140

I heard soft clattering of chains as women gathered around me. I felt a pussy shoved into my face and heard, "Eat me, girl."

I crawled closer between her legs on my knees and pressed my lips to her labia lips. I licked and sucked on my her engorged skin. My tongue snaked between the labia lips to caress her innermost recesses. I was not skilled but I could feel when she was getting close to orgasm. I slowed my assault, knowing that increased pleasure came from prolonging the stimulation. Finally, she grabbed the back of my head. She pulled it into her groin hard and shouting "Now, I'm coming." And come she did. It was an enormous orgasm. The churning convulsions rumbled on and on for what seemed like hours. I could hear the smile in her voice when she said, "That was amazing. Your tongue ring was wonderful. I climaxed faster and harder than ever before. I'm going to playing with you over and over."

My face was wet with her love juices. I said," Thank you, Mistress. I'm glad I pleased you."

I heard another girl say, "My turn, get out of there Amelia." I felt her back away. She was quickly replaced by another. I gave ten slave girls great orgasms by the time they stopped. All of them praised my tongue stud for making me "The Best."

The bar was raised, standing me up. It felt so good to be touched.

It was an incredible feeling. So many women touching me in the most pleasant, stimulating way. The fingers dipped into my pussy and I felt arousal spreading through me. Soon I was gasping and pleading with them to do it harder, faster, deeper. I came with a great gush of love juice down my legs. I slumped and hung from my wrists until someone lifted me. "Don't stop, mistresses, Please don't stop."

They didn't stop. The hands moved around. Someone else started kissing me. I had four wonderful orgasms before they stopped. No one said a word the whole time.

Someone released my chain from above. Several sets of hands walked me across the room until my hips were stopped by a horizontal wooden bar. My feet were tied down and I was bent forward over the bar until I was horizontal. My chain was fastened in front of me, holding me trapped against the bar.

I was aroused beyond all experience. I moaned and writhed in my chains. My loins burned. I was ready to be taken. I needed to know if my new equipment functioned as well as the girls I had just made climax. I was so hot. I needed to climax again. I was needy. I realized I needed to have a man in me. I needed to be fucked, hard. My pussy was sopping. I could feel my love juices running down my leg. I moaned and it turned into a scream of pleasure as fingers stroked my pussy. I screamed and pleaded to be fucked over and over. I was in desperate need and knew I would die of denial.

Suddenly a huge cock plunged into my sopping cunt. It was a fitting climax to a surprising and increasingly wonderful set of events. I was taken to heaven with two strokes of this cock. I climaxed again and again as he pumped me up. Finally, I felt him come in me. His hot seed flowed into me like a geyser. I instantly climaxed my final time. It was overwhelming. It was glorious . I fainted. When I awoke, I was empty and still fastened over the bar. I was drained and happy. I was more content to be a slave than I ever expected. I wanted my sight back, but I didn't care about my chains any more. I had never felt this good when I was a free man. I wanted more and if it took being a helpless female slave to get it, I was game.

Someone freed my chain and I raised up. My feet were untied and I was led to the bath. I really needed cleaning.

"Good time, Rayna?"

"Yes, Mistress. Surprisingly, I loved every minute of it, even the whip."

She cleaned me up and took me back to my concrete bed. I didn't mind being there this time. I just wanted to sleep. Lagina was in "My cell" when I was returned. She was chained to a separate ring and sound asleep on a mat. Her arms were different.

Mistress locked my tether on me and removed my leash. Then she fixed my arms like Lagina. They were pulled high

143

on my back and locked to the tether chain. She pulled them high and tight. They were strained and would ache shortly. She said, "This is how your hands will be fastened when they aren't needed. Your tendons will stretch and it will be more comfortable later." Then she left and locked the cell door.

I looked at Lagina, but we were fastened far enough apart we couldn't cuddle, though I needed it. I lay on my mast and slept.

In the morning Rayna and I were both awake, hoping for breakfast when Mistress approached. We were already kneeling as required and we straightened up when we heard Mistress' footsteps approaching. I adjusted my posture as erect and proud as I was taught.

"Good morning, Lagina. Are you ready for another adventure?"

"Oh yes, Mistress. I am so bored here, even a whipping sounds good."

"Be careful what you wish for Lagina."

"Yes, Mistress."

"Today I'm taking you to meet my master."

"You really have a master, Mistress?"

"All the girls will, Lagina. Female emancipation does not exist here. Although every man is your Master, usually girls here are sold to a man so she has a personal master. That's what all the graduates say they want. I believe them because that's what I want and have. I have a personal master and that's who I am taking you to see. "

"Oh. Can you tell me anything more?"

"No need. All you will ever need to know is obey your masters and never speak without permission. Also, give him all the pleasure you can."

I was fed and bathed. Mistress put a hood on me then led me out of the cell and a long distance away. When I felt a soft surface under my feet she ordered me to kneel. I don't know why, but I felt instant lust. I was aroused as hell and all I did was kneel.

A male voice said, "Katy, your charge seems to be in good order. How is she doing?"

Now I knew. I had gone into arousal just by being near a man. Or was it because I knew he was a master?

"Master, Lagina is progressing ahead of schedule. She did not know she was a natural submissive and it took her a few days to learn that. Since then her obedience and acceptance have improved at a faster rate. She is about ready for formal skills training."

"Excellent, Katy. Show me how she reacts under discipline."

Uh Oh. Not so good, I guess. I was ready to roll over and spread my legs and I was getting disciplined!

"Mistress said, "Lagina. You are going to be whipped. Raise up high on your knees and put your forehead on the floor."

"Yes, Mistress." I put myself as directed. I resolved not to scream.

The first fiery stroke scalded my ass. I flinched, but didn't make a sound. I think I was getting used to a red ass. The blow didn't hurt as it had before. I knew I wouldn't die from it. "One, Thank you Mistress."

"Two, Thank you Mistress." The second stroke didn't hurt. It was pure pleasure. I was ready to climax.

The third stroke landed square on my upraised ass. It was glorious. I don't know why I ever feared a whipping. This was beyond pleasure. It was heavenly. I climaxed loudly. My scream of pleasure vibrated in my ears. I felt my love juices flowing down my belly. I was chagrined at how easily I was forced to climax. I was thrilled to have such a wonderful orgasm. "Three,.. Mistress. Th..Thank you," I stumbled

The fourth stoke landed on my upper thigh and drove me back up the mountain toward another climax. It was heavenly. I moaned, "Four Mistress...Thank...you."

146

The fifth stroke hit just below my waist. It was the best one yet. I screamed with my second huge orgasm and nearly collapsed with my spasming belly. I managed to stay in position, barely. "F...Five, ..Mistress, Th..Thank you so much."

She waited and let me regain some measure of composure before her next blow landed on my ass. It shoved me back up to my peak of arousal. I was ready to come again. "Six. Thank you mistress."

"That's enough, Katy. You have trained her well. Good Job."

I hadn't moved through all six strokes and two huge orgasms. I was still so aroused I had trouble thinking of anything but his wonderful cock.

"Thank you, Master," I could hear the relief and pride in her voice. Hell, I felt proud of my resolve too. I was glad I had shown up well for Mistress." I know. I know. I was ashamed I had given in. I was a slave and happy to obey. I was even glad to accept a whipping to help my Mistress. How low I had sunk. And I was still aroused.

Is this all it took to enslave a woman. I wasn't a whiny, dependent woman. I was educated and once a Queen in a male dominated world. I had shown I could prevail over many men. After a few short weeks of chains and pain I wouldn't say boo to any man or woman. Mistress had broken me to heel. I was a bitch in heat. I wanted the attention and praise of my Mistress so much, I would do anything. I wanted my master to take me now, hard. My helpless arousal in his presence and the pleasure of the whip destroyed my strength. I used to think of myself as tough. I was putty in anyone's hands now. I don't think I can ever recover. I know I am a slave. Mistress knows it and now so does the man she calls Master.

He said," Lagina, what will you do if I remove your hood?"

Remove my hood? Would he? Oh God, I want it off so bad. "Master, I will do anything you want. Command me."

"Lagina. I already own you. You will do anything I tell you to do or suffer the consequences. Aren't you offering me what I already have?"

"Master, of course I will obey you. If you choose to remove the hood and let me see again, I will willingly serve you and do my best to please you. The willing obedience of a woman can be more rewarding than simple obedience."

"Are you offering to love me if I return your sight?"

"I will more than love you master. I will make your joy my masterwork. I will bend every waking moment to finding new ways to please you." I didn't think about these words. They flowed unbidden from me. I would more than love anyone who gave me sight again."

"All right. I will test this claim of yours. Katy, would you please remove her hood. Lagina, close your eyes."

I felt the hood removed. I kept my eyes closed.

"How do you feel Lagina?"

"Fine Master, may I open them, please?" Then fuck me, please.


He was gorgeous, tall, dark haired and with a great body. He fucked me well. He gave me two orgasms and then his climax and my third one happened together.

Mistress took me back to the cell I now shared with Rayna. After she fastened the tether to the back of my collar, she released my wrists and pulled them up high on my back and locked them to the tether chain. I was sure she tightened them more than last night. The ache in my shoulders and upper arms started immediately. The reverse prayer position. I hope she was right that I would adjust so it didn't hurt. Soon, please.

# Chapter 13 : Adjustments

Master came to our cell and put hoods on both of us. The he took us out on nose leashes. We walked for a few minutes before he stopped us. He moved us apart and said, "Don't move."

I froze. I heard him moving about and scrapes and clinks. Then he said, "Lagina, leash."

I tilted my head back and stuck out my tongue. I felt him clip a chain onto my tongue ring. More clinking and the chain on my tongue pulled hard and I stretched as high as I could. It stopped and I was hanging from my tongue on tiptoe. Then I heard him do the same thing to Rayna. He came back to me. I felt the air move on my naked breasts. He did something near my face, only touching my strained tongue lightly twice.

In a minute he was back to me. I felt something probing my cunt, then a large, fat dildo slid into me. It stopped just short of the end of my love canal. He went away and I heard Rayna's exclamation as presumably the same thing was done to her. He walked away again.

I heard a hum and felt the dildo start a faint vibration and it was faintly arousing, but not strong enough to make me climax. He left me alone after that. Some time later, my toes were tired and I lowered them just a little, forcing the dildo a little farther into me. When I lowered, my tongue stretched more and I found something wonderful. My clit ring began to vibrate fiercely. This would give me a climax soon. I felt my arousal grow. But my tongue was hurting so I got on my tiptoes again. My clit stopped getting the vibrations and my toes were hurting. Soon I was slowly rising and falling, trying to find that timing that would let me climax and not pull my tongue out by its roots. I was moaning and whimpering, but I didn't care. It was so damn frustrating. I couldn't stay in contact with the vibrator long enough to climax. I was so close. Another ten seconds I thought, but I was probably wrong.

I heard Rayna making the same sort of noises mixed with what sounded like strangled profanity. She must be on a similar tongue stretcher as me. This wasn't just punishment. This device had another purpose. I guessed wanted to stretch our tongues. I wasn't sure why. Maybe to make us freaks and subject us to a different kind of humiliation? Maybe so we could do an even better job eating cats. Maybe they would sell us to a woman or open a brothel for women to come and get eaten out by the two most accomplished cat eaters on the planet?

I heard swish, thwack and I felt the pain spreading through my ass. Master was whipping me too. Oh no. I'd rip my tongue out. A long pause and another stripe. Then I realized, she was hurrying me toward an orgasm. The heat flowed through my bottom straight to my pussy. It was

151

flaming now. Just one more, I thought. But it never came. Mistress walked to Rayna and gave her two strokes too. then he walked away.

We were left on the devices for hours, pumping up and down like slow motion Jack-In-The-Boxes. I could tell from the feel of my pussy and the rivulets on my legs that I was keeping the shaft well lubricated. Every stroke I had the same thought: If only I could go a little lower, I could climax. I kept stretching down as far as I could. I accidentally found that if I leaned forward too, my clit could reach the vibrator. I managed to maintain body contact with the vibrator just long enough to climax. Hallelujah. My orgasm finally washed over me and I screamed my pleasure for all to hear. I'm sure my tongue must be an inch longer than when I started.

I had to keep up my motion after the climax. I was driven by the pain in my toes and my tongue. After Rayna had climaxed, Master came and did something near my tongue again. He went to Rayna and in a moment took her down. He came back and took me down too. I was glad to have that over with. My tongue was sore and I was thirsty and hungry. Master squirted a little water in my mouth and boy was it good.

He took us somewhere else and made us kneel.

I heard squeals of pleasure and giggles then we were claimed by a flock of girls. We were desert, I guess. I had to eat out

152

ten girls before they stopped coming.  I guess there may have been some repeaters there, but how would I know.  They all tasted very similar.  not the same, but close.

A girl would step close and take hold of my nose ring.  She'd lift my nose and order me to stick out my tongue.  They were very appreciative and said nice things about it.  Then they'd pull my nose into her crotch and order me to make her come.  I was getting real good at eating cat.  My tongue ring seemed to drive them to orgasm quickly.  When I finished a girl, someone would wipe my face with a wet cloth.  I needed it.  Girls are not tidy when they come.  I felt like I was being sprayed with a hose.

When they were done they ordered me to do one more.  They laid Rayna on her back and had me do her.  She came quickly.  Finally it was my turn.  Rayna and I traded places and she gave me a humungous climax.  Her tongue was fantastic.  Long, strong, and with her ring it was beautifully unbearable. He took us back to our cell and put our food bowls on the floor. He held our leashes while we ate.  Then he did something different.  He tethered us to the same wall ring.  Our wrists were still hastened high on our backs so they were not usable.  He wiped the food off our nose rings and took the leashes off. He said, "You two can play with each other if you want." Then he left and closed the cell door behind him.

Rayna and I were kneeling, facing each other.

Rayna said, "Do you want to be first?"

We romped and played like new puppies. It was so good to be able to play with each other. Rayna went nuts when I was on top and sucked her nipple. She is so sensitive one lick drives her crazy. Mine are very sensitive too. I wonder if the rings make them more sensitive? I've noticed that my nipples are rock hard all the time. I think the way the rings are always moving arouses them. Of course being sucked is fantastic.

We didn't get much sleep that night, but I felt wonderful the next day. I even caught Rayna humming as we knelt waiting for Master.

Master came and took us back to the shop again. This time the smith hung bells on every one of our rings. The bells all hung from short chains below our rings. We tinkled at every move. He even put a big bell on each anklet and bracelet. The bells all hung on short chains below the rings.

Nothing hurt, but the bells were loud and shaming. I couldn't move without ringing one or more bells. Walking I sounded like a sleigh horse. People belled cats to give the mice a chance. I was belled to ensure I could do nothing without notice. It was a great way to ensure maximum humiliation by the largest number of people. Everyone would watch the naked slave girl walking on her leash. Helpless and despised and even envied, judging from some of the female looks I saw.

154

Rayna and I had our tongues stretched every other day followed by our 'tongue exercise' with all the other girls. I have to admit I liked it too. It was one way to make friends. Sometimes Master left the hood off so I could see them. They were all beautiful and I was envious because they only received punishment when they broke a rule. Rayna and I were here to be punished. After our bells were installed, Master took us to a new room. She told us, "This room is where we keep the 'Horse.' It is only used for serious punishment."

He opened the door and led us in. The room was high and dark. He turned on a light. I saw a structure like a steep roof about three feet high and only a foot wide sitting just off the floor. He clipped my leash to a wall ring and led Rayna to one end of the seven or eight foot long roof. He led Rayna to straddle it, walk forward a foot or so, and slide her hobble chain under it. He clipped her leash to a ring in the middle of the roof. Master put me on the other end. Because of the roof being wider at the bottom, my hobble was pretty tight. So far this didn't look bad at all. I guess we had to sit on this thing, but it was so low we could just stand up if it was uncomfortable.

Mistress pulled both our leashes tighter to the ring in the middle of the roof thingy and tied them off. We both had to lean far forward. He asked, "Comfy, girls?"

We both said, "Yes, Master."

155

Master went to a box on the wall, opened a cover and the thing we were sitting on rose farther off the ground. It got higher until my feet left the ground and all the weight of my body was resting on my pussy. My hobble chain was somehow caught on a hook or something on the ground so my feet were unable to lift. They were only able to pull me down harder on the top of the roof. Suddenly both Rayna and I were in pain. The narrow top of the roof was pressing hard into my pussy. I cried out, "Master. This is too hard. Its going to cut me in half."

Rayna whimpered something about it being terrible. We both were crying. We couldn't move and the pain in my pussy was horrible. I was sure it would kill me.

Master said. This is the 'Horse. It has a reputation for doing wonders for a disobedient girl. Remember, though, you're here to b punished. I'll see you later. He turned off the light and closed the door. We whimpered and cried in the dark. I said, "Rayna, I'm sure this won't kill us. The King wants us to live and be punished forever."

She said, "[sob] You must be right Lagina. [sob] They don't want to kill us. But I don't think, [sob], he would mind overmuch if they did. [sob]"

We were both quiet except for our various pitiful noises. We didn't want to talk. The pain was too great for thinking or even singing. The dark was oppressive. We were left on the horse so long I thought we were going to be left there ll night.

Master opened the door at long last and turned on the light. I looked at Rayna. Her eyes were red with the tears that had mostly dried on her face. She looked as pained and tired as I felt. Master lowered the horse and the pain diminished as we could stand on our feet again. He untied our leashes and backed us off the horse. He let us walk at our own pace. I could barely waddle along. I was afraid my legs were permanently bowed from that awful ride. I was hurting down below and wondered if I could ever feel pleasure there again.

I asked him, "Master, will that have a lasting effect?"

He laughed and said, "Hurts a lot doesn't it. You'll be good as new tomorrow. You'll get your tongue exercise then and you'll see. Your girl parts are tougher than you think."

Our routine had settled into a pattern. one day we'd get exercise , training in slave girl stuff, and a tongue stretching/cat eating exercise. The next day we'd get exercise, some slave girl stuff, then a punishment. Today was punishment.

Now we spend most of our time with our hands hoisted high on our backs. Master had been right. They didn't hurt anymore and he pulled them higher all the time. Now my fingers touched my collar . I would probably have them locked directly on my collar in a week. They were useless up there, but we didn't need them for sex or punishment and that seemed to be the extent of our lives, for now at least.

# Chapter 14 : Labeled

After feeding us, Master took us to the shop again. I had become accustomed to my bells and found them comforting rather than demeaning, though if someone else saw me I was embarrassed. Strangely, that embarrassment almost always turned into arousal. I really don't understand my body.

We already had tight steel bands around our waists. They had several attachment rings spaced around them. The smith added small chains circled my upper thighs and joined them to the outside of the waist belt. In front there was a small clip on the chain positioned perfectly so they could grasp and pull my labia rings apart, exposing my inner lips, my most secret place.

Short chains were placed on my nipple rings with spring clips on the dangling ends. The chains were just long enough to clip onto the other nipple ring, I didn't understand their purpose and said so.

Master walked up to me and said, "Watch." He took one clip in his hand and used the other to pull down on my leash, forcing me to bend my head forward. When I had bent far enough, he clipped the end of the chain onto my nose ring. He did the same with my other chain.

He released my leash and said, "Lift your head until it hurts."

I lifted my head only an inch or so. The lifting of my nipples by their rings as well as the pull on my nose were getting painful.

He fitted them to Rayna and clipped the new labia clips on to our labia rings, opening us to view.

Master said, "These are training devices to teach you not to look at a master or mistress without orders." He removed them from my nose ring and after Rayna had hers installed we were strapped to the wall again. A new man came in with a rolling cart of equipment. He was heavily tattooed and Master took him aside and showed him some papers. The man heartily agreed and came back to us. He said, "I'm going to put some ink on both of you. One of you want to go first or shall I choose?"

We were silent and he turned to me with his needle in hand. I shivered, but I couldn't run and hide. I was curious what Master had in mind, anyway. It hurt but less than the whip. I couldn't move anyway so I was still. In the end I got three words put on me in a black Gothic type: "Submit" on my left breast, "Obey" on my right breast, and "Slave" above my cunt. They were all true, but I hated them anyway. Just as well no one cared what I thought. Rayna got exactly the same words in the same places. She cried. I guess she hated them too.

Master led us back to our cell. He put the nipple to nose chains on us. All the new chains made it uncomfortable to walk.  Both of them pulled at every step.  With my head bent so far I couldn't see far enough ahead to avoid other people or any obstacles above floor level.  I felt vulnerable and exposed as well as labeled.  More humiliating, I guess.

Master left the nipple chains on our noses the rest of the day and only took them off when it was our bed time.

Rayna and I always slept with our hands locked high on our back.  I was getting used to it and it they didn't ache any more.  Now my fingers reached higher than my collar.  In a short time Master would be able to lock my wrists directly to my collar.  I don't suppose this was important to anyone but me, but it felt like it should be.

Master kept putting us in the tongue stretcher room every other day, alternating between that and some form of punishment.  Our tongues were getting unusually long and strong.  I was now able to touch the bridge of my nose with the tip of my tongue.  So could Rayna.  And they were much stronger than normal, I guess because after the stretching we each gave ten or so climaxes to the other girls.  We licked a lot.

Our least favorite non-punishment was the weekly parade.  One day a week all the girls would be lined up and put in a coffle.  Four feet of chain would be locked to a girls collar and thence to another girl.  All twenty odd girls would be joined in a single file.  All our hands would be locked high on our backs and, of course we were naked and hobbled. Tasha would be first on the coffle The male trainers would lead us outside and walk us all around the compound. Free women, clothed and unrestrained and men would come and watch us. They would talk among themselves and point as we walked past. Often some would come close and touch or fondle us. We would walk until the trainers stopped us for a group to inspect.

Sometimes some of the girls would be borrowed for a private party or as a loan to a customer. The parade was a chance for the ones who arranged such things to inspect the merchandise. We had to obey every order from any free person. It wasn't unusual for a girl to have to give a blow job or eat a cat. Usually it was just to assume a pose. I think it was an important part of our training to show us we had to obey everyone, not just our trainers. It made a strong impression on me and, I think, especially Rayna.

It was especially humiliating when we were put in the parade with our nipple chains clipped to our nose rings. I couldn't see anything but the girl's feet in front of me. Even this was note worthy because only Rayna and I were shod. Our high heels were locked on our feet so we were made tall and made to bow our heads. I am sure Master was watching and smiled every time a free woman tweaked one of my nose-to-nipple chains. It happened a lot because Rayna and I were "Different."

# Chapter 15 : Pillory

One of Master's favorite punishments for Lagina and I was the pillory. Our hands and neck fit perfectly if unlocked. The chains to our wrists were just long enough. After exercise he would lock us into the solid oak pillory. Our feet were held at maximum separation by the board we had to walk around before bending over. Once the bar was lowered we were fucked in every hole for hours. Usually Master would put a blindfold on us before locking our heads down. Them he would use the attached head strap to pull my head back so my mouth was readily accessible. There were two pillories mounted side by side so we could talk if we weren't being used.

My user could be either a man or woman. We were in a good position for eating a girl's cat. I think Mistress wanted to make sure we were experienced with women. I think she used me a lot herself because she had a distinctive perfume and she tasted spicy. I can't be sure, but she was a joy to eat. Most times the men would whip my ass before using me. I'm sure it made them hard to hear my squeals and moans. I came to enjoy a good whipping too. If they did it right, hard strokes with a good space between them, I got aroused and it they gave me more than four strokes, I was likely to come. It was good for them too because it warmed me up and got me well lubricated. Whatever the Docs had done to me, I enjoyed sex and I flowed like a geyser. If I had ever been allowed clothing, I would have soiled it every day.

This was becoming a pleasant life. There was much to be said for copious sex and no responsibility. Sure the punishments were nasty, but usually that was of limited duration. What we were receiving were regular doses of unpleasant but bearable pain lasting for part of a day. The really long term punishment was the many, many ways Master had found to put the taste of unbearable humiliation in my mouth all the time. I think that was worst for Lagina too. I liked being a royal Prince that almost everyone respected and feared. I had lost all of that when I was made female. Everything else, the rings, bells, chains, and my tongue, had me in free fall. I don't know how far down I can go. I only hope People who see what I have become in the future, won't recognize me. I surely don't resemble Ramalah now, but the King will likely enjoy showing people why they shouldn't cross him.

One of my greatest surprises was anal sex. I knew it was practiced in my part of the world, but I had never done it. The first time Master had locked me in the pillory I felt someone rubbing lubricant on and in my asshole. I wanted to say, "Excuse me, you've got the wrong hole." I didn't because I would have gotten a beating for speaking without permission. I'm glad I didn't, because it wasn't unpleasant. I guess I knew I was a slave girl by then, because I actually felt glad to have been able to please a man. Since then I've been buggered a thousand times and I enjoy it. I'm almost always able to get aroused and climax along with my user. A couple of times I think I was taken in the ass by a girl using a strap-on dildo, because my user's voice was high pitched and didn't climax in me. From the sounds she made I think she climaxed but I didn't feel it. Oh well, I live to serve.

I'm always relaxed when I'm in the pillory. There's absolutely nothing I can do. I'm immobile, just a piece of sex furniture for anyone to use. As I wait for my next user, I imagine an electronic screen in the hallway like they have in airports showing arrivals and departures. This one would have at least two entries. One for each pillory and maybe more for each device available. It shows Rayna on Pillory One and Lagina on pillory two. It would show how long we'd been locked in place, the number of users, which hole got used and how many strokes of the whip or cane. Some days the scoreboard would show how many orgasms I'd had and number of times my user orgasmed. I was sure I got more.

I've come to like the sounds of my bells. They are usually a good indicator of my state of excitement. In the pillory I couldn't move anything but my butt and even that was well constrained by my securely fastened head, wrists and feet. Nevertheless, my bells sounded loud when I was being ridden. Even my nipple bells sounded of. As My user impaled me, my breasts would sway in circles knocking against each other and causing the bells to shake. Thee closer I get to orgasm, the louder they ring. I don't know why. I must tense up or something as I get more aroused. Of course the bells hanging from my labia lips and clit are the loudest of all. The smith used bells of slightly different tone for those in my loins than those in my breasts. The loin rings were just a little sharper. When the clips are used to keep my labia lips spread the sounds are a little less. I think its because the bells rub against my legs sometimes. I never get to watch them but I do feel them on the sensitive skin of my inner thighs.

Its not unusual for the men enjoying my loins, either hole, to grasp my dangling breasts and pull them as they thrust. Sort of love handles for the men. Sometimes it hurts because they hold them too tight or pull too hard. My cries of pain usually work to lessen the pain. I guess if I was used by a real sadist my yelps would cause him to make it worse. So far its worked the way I prefer, that is, less pain. I guess the risk of falling into harsh hands is part of the thrill I feel when I'm first locked in place. I do feel excited when even the tiny bit of freedom I have is taken away. Usually it results in multiple orgasms without me having to choose or worry. Its never my decision. I guess I've learned to accept a slave's lot.

# Chapter 16 : Milking

Our days always began and ended the same way. We were cleaned inside and out, then we were fed. Next was an exercise session followed by several forced orgasms and then training, punishment and our afternoon feeding. Never anything to eat at lunch so we were ravenous by the afternoon feeding.

All of the places we were taken had cameras mounted behind one way bubbles. I accepted we were recorded and observed by unseen eyes. Sometimes I could feel eyes on me, but I never knew for sure. It was comforting to think that my master might be watching me. That thought always made me try especially hard to be graceful and elegant in my poses and motions.

Often training time included a milking session. Until my first milking, I didn't even know this existed. That first day, Master led me to a stand or structure made out of steel pipe. He said, "I'm going to milk you now, Lagina. Most girls enjoy this."

I didn't know what he meant. I was not producing any milk, and had never done so. What were they going to do? He held on to my leash, pulling me forward with one hand. He put his other hand on my ass, not pushing, but guiding and feeling me. Quite nice. He guided me to the center of the structure. Then forward until my ankles were trapped in two

U-shaped fixtures on a cross bar only inches off the floor. I felt them close around my ankles, trapping them. He dropped my leash and raised a bar until my thighs were resting against it. He pulled my leash down, and my torso followed until my shoulders rested on another cross bar. A short chain from the crossbar was clipped to my collar so I couldn't raise up. He dropped the leash, put a blindfold, and a ball gag on me. My head was a little lower than my ass. I felt straps put on both knees and then pulled wide apart and fastened.

I wriggled and confirmed I was securely fastened, again. I wasn't going to fight. I was sure he wasn't going to hurt me, but I was curious what was going to happen to me now. I felt my breasts wiped with a damp cloth and a heavy bra was put around my chest. I felt soft cups snug around my breasts held on by a strap across my back. I couldn't see anything or move anything. I reveled in my helplessness. I felt so submissive. Soothing hands rubbed my back and ass, playing up and down my thighs. I felt like a prize cow being soothed before the milking, I guess I was. I was tense when I was first fastened in the machine. Blind, mute, helpless. The hands relaxed me until I felt soft, pliant.

I heard a pump start and felt my breasts and tits being sucked into the cups of the bra. And then released in a slow rhythm – one breast at a time. I could feel my pussy starting to moisten and my tits getting increasingly sensitive. I closed my eyes, and relaxed into the pumping feeling. It was very tense and exciting. My legs started to shake and I developed goose pimples all over. My pussy was trembling and I was aroused, but I couldn't get close to an orgasm. I discovered if I shook my ass sideways, my clit ring stimulated me. Again, I got closer to an orgasm, but not close enough. My breasts felt wonderful, but not enough.


Milking time was one of my great pleasures. The milking machine was like the pillory. It held the girl immobile, just waiting for me. But when I started the pump, it aroused her so she was incredibly responsive. It did the foreplay. I started the process by running my hands all over her, gently, just touching her silky smooth skin and reveling in her possession. When she felt relaxed I started the pump and for a minute watched the rhythmic kneading of her breasts. I wanted to do that, but the machine was more gentle. After it ran for a minute or two, my cock was hard. Ready, I would place it on her pussy and like magic, she would spread open her labia lips and invite me in. She was hot and slippery, open and trembling with eagerness. I would start slow. I didn't want to come too soon. I wanted to enjoy her whole milking cycle.

I knew she wanted me to speed up and give her release by the way she moaned through her gag. I enjoyed her frustration and delighted in teasing her. I knew her orgasm would be stronger if I delayed a little. She was strapped tightly and couldn't do anything but wriggle. When she trembled around me and her moans turned to whimpers, I knew she had come to a boil. I sped up and she came in a surge. I felt her hot love juices flow around my cock and leak past our imperfect seal. I wasn't ready yet so I pumped harder and grabbed her around her waist. I came and filled her with my spend. She came again on my heels and we filled her like a balloon. I withdrew, cleaned myself with a damp cloth and patted her ass. She only produced enough milk to coat the tubes. Not enough to drink. I knew this would improve the more she was milked. I hoped her milk would be good. Once she got going she was going to beg to be milked every day.

Then, oh joy, I felt probing fingers at my pussy. They stroked down one lip then up the other. Yes. This was going to do it if only they kept going. I prayed they would keep it up just a little longer, but hey left me. My joy turned to ashes in that instant. They were just teasing me. I was so needy. I sobbed into my bit. wishing I could plead with him to continue. I struggled in my bonds, but I couldn't budge anything. I was helpless in my need. I moaned in loss. Then the fingers returned. They stroked me into fiery arousal and this time his cock entered my sopping pussy. I couldn't move a muscle. It was up to him. He thrust in easily and slowly withdrew, In and out, slow, languid. I needed him to speed up. I couldn't orgasm unless he moved faster. Oh how I wished I could speak, He couldn't see my face or my need. I was an immobile, mute female form. My frustration knew no bounds. I whimpered, hoping he would understand.

Miracle of miracles. I think he understood. He sped up and my arousal flew to the very edge and blossomed into a stupendous orgasm. I screamed and pleaded for mercy then moaned in unbearable pleasure as my belly jumped and trembled with scalding heat and love juices poured in to my sex as I came again and again in uncountable, endlessly repeating orgasms. And they were huge. Every muscle in my body spasmed in a paroxysm of joy. If he felt anything from my tight held body, it was my internal muscles contracting around him. Vainly trying to keep him in me. I couldn't tell if he felt anything because he kept pumping, instantly causing my arousal to grow. Meanwhile the machine kept on pumping my boobs, and how good that felt. I felt my arousal climbing high. All I could do was moan my pleasure. I hope he understood how happy I was to feel him in me. I had no idea who he was. I wished I could see him, kiss him, use my arms to love him properly. It came to me while he was pumping me up to an orgasm. Slave girls do not make love. They are given orgasms when their owners think they deserve it, or for their own pleasure. I was good with that. I'm a slave girl now, I think. I've been packaged as men want me, I'm helpless, and I've had the best orgasm of my life. My life was complete.

Then he came in me and his hot spend flowed through me. I climaxed again while his spend was fresh and our mixed fluids flowed down my legs. The wonderful machine kept pumping my breasts. Whoever he was, he withdrew from me, patted my ass and left without a word. I hoped it was Alex. Even if I couldn't be with him, I hoped I had pleasured him.

Twenty minutes later, he stopped the machine. He took the bra off. My nipples were so sensitive I almost screamed as my rings swayed in them. I felt like any touch – however light and where ever applied – would make me come in a tremendous orgasm. My mind was filled with the tense excitement emanating from the two very hard spots on my chest. A sort of long purr crept from my throat and past my gag.

# Chapter 17 : Ajax

The worst humiliation of all began as a normal day. Lagina and I were cleaned and fed then were exercised and trained in belly dance. That was actually more fun than work. The instructor was another slave. We spent a couple of hours learning some simple steps and practicing moving our breasts in time to the music. It was a lot of pectoral exercise We couldn't do much in that time, but we learned the exercises to control our breasts. I'm sure we would be required to practice those until we had full control. It was how they did things here.

Master locked our hands to our collars and put leashes on our nose rings. He led us out of the building and into the grassy yard between buildings. I saw a group of men and a few clothed women clustered together in front of us. As we approached Master called out, "Hi. Here to see the performance? It may take some time."

The people parted for us and then I saw it. It was instantly horrible in its implications. Several people were touching it calling to its inhabitant. I saw it all too clearly. It was a cage made of thick steel bars with many crosspieces. Too low to stand upright in and plenty wide enough for many people to lie in it. It held a dog. A large, friendly dog. Master said, to us, "Girls, this is Ajax. You need to be nice to him."

Master unlocked the massive padlock. He ordered, "Kneel."

Both of us obeyed. He unlocked our hands so we could reach a little way in front of our waist. "Crawl in."

We both crawled in the open door. He closed and locked it. "Ajax is well trained and very friendly. You will stay in here until he has fucked both of you. I freed your hands so you can help him. All these people are here to watch. If you get it done quickly they will tell me and I'll let you out. If you're fucked and no one sees you, then you'll have to do it again. Make sure you have an audience."

My body cringed at the thought. Both of us backed up against the bars and clamped our legs together. Master slid a bowl of water into the cage and said, "Have fun."

We both stared at the big dog. He was sitting on his haunches looking expectantly at us.

Master said, "Use you hands to get him stiff then he'll do you doggy style." He walked away.

I looked at Rayna and said, "It shouldn't be any worse the being in the pillory and we like that."

Rayna said, "No way. I'll rot in here before I left him in me. That's disgusting."

"Right," I said, "they won't let us die in here. Any amount of pain is better than helping a dog screw you."

We looked at each other and the dog. He looked back, waiting for us to do something. Eventually we had to pee. We decided on a corner to use and we took turns squatting there. When we were done Ajax went and smelled our urine and he peed there too. This was the first chance we had to see his penis. It was big. Long and thick, it looked just like a man's penis.

I said, "You know, it looks like the ones we usually have in us."

Rayna replied, "You'll have puppies."

I snorted, " Impossible. but I'll probably have an orgasm. I'd like an orgasm about now."

Master came out at dusk and gave us a blanket. We huddled under it to sleep. I was still very cold that night until Ajax came over and lay beside me. He Licked my face and I went to sleep.

Master came out at first light and took away our blanket. He said, The audience will be back in a little while. Be sure someone sees you do it or it won't count.

We both said, "Yes, Master."

I asked, "Master, will we be fed out here?"

He replied, "I will put a bowl of food and a bowl of water in there twice a day. You'll have to share with Ajax."

We sat and looked at Ajax. The idea of him fucking me seemed better now than yesterday. After all, he was a male mammal. I was a female mammal. Our sex parts were compatible. We both liked sex. I wanted out of here pretty badly now. I looked at Rayna. She looked somehow softer.

I said, "I'm about ready to try it. How about you?

Rayna looked at me and said, I'd rather have you love me." She leaned over and kissed me. We usually have sex with each other at night. Last night I felt like Ajax was a chaperone and I didn't want to do it. Now, her kiss made me horny as hell. I laid her down and stuck my nose in her cunt. I licked and sucked and she must have been horny too, because she came after only seven or eight licks. Her moans and final scream filled the yard.

When she recovered I said, "My turn bitch. Get up."

She raised on one hand and said, "Well, get your ass on the ground, Bitch, and spread 'em."

We traded places and her amazing tongue took me to heaven in seconds. Damn, we were good.

I said, 'Thank you, my talented, beautiful Princess."

Rayna said, "You're welcome, your majesty."

I saw we had a small audience and said, "Ajax, here boy."

He trotted over and I stroked his penis. He sprang to life immediately and barked, followed by a low growl.

I took his meaning and rolled over. I lifted my ass in the air and waggled it. I felt his stiff prick at my pussy and reached back to align him. I was already sopping and he slid right in. He was just as big and long as many of the men who'd been in me before him. He pumped and got me very aroused. He came and filled me with hot juices and I orgasmed immediately, completely filling me and squirting out on the ground.

Rayna applauded and said, "Good boy, Ajax. You too slut."

I said, It was pretty good, Bitch. You should try him. I bet he can do you right now."

Ajax walked away and I said, "Be nice to him. He wants you. I can see it in his eyes. Let him smell your cunt. Its still wet from your orgasm. I bet it gets him stiff."

Rayna looked at me and said, "Crazy Bitch." But she crawled to Ajax and stuck her cunt in his nose. He sniffed then licked her. His long tongue slipped inside her and she moaned, then said, "Damn. His tongue is about as good as yours."

"Is he hard"

She felt his dick and said, "As a rock." She pivoted on one knee and put her head on the ground and ass in the air. Ajax put his front paws on her back and rammed his packer straight into her. She didn't have to guide him. I guess I was good practice.

She moaned some more and that caused Ajax to bay. It was startling but a heartfelt expression of pleasure from both of them. I watched her face. It began focused and slowly relaxed into pure pleasure. She didn't care who or what was in her right now. She was just getting that unique female pleasure of having something in her and making her orgasm. And Orgasm she did, with a scream of pleasure and a bark from Ajax. He came a moment later and I watched their merged love juices squirt out of her and dribble onto the ground.

There was a round of applause and congratulations from our audience. I was drawn back to the reality and was humiliated anew. A dozen men and women had watched us be fucked by a dog. And we both showed pleasure at our taking. I sat against the bars and strained to cover my face with my pinioned arms. I could only get my fingers to my chin before I remembered to bow my head. I knew it was too late. Rayna's and my joyful expressions while Ajax took us were undoubtedly recorded and ready to be shown to anyone the King wished. Shit.

Master came and took us out of the cage to the applause of the audience. He locked our hands to our collars, put the leashes on our nose rings, and led us back inside. He took us to the bath and cleaned us off. We were fed and taken to exercise class. Another day started.

# Chapter 18 : Puppies

At lights out Master told us that tomorrow we would start animal play. We were going to be puppy girls. He wanted us to try and play at actually being a puppy. To try and feel what a real puppy would feel. A weak tiny puppy. Totally dependent on him for everything yet playful, curious and eager to please.

Rayna asked, "Master, why are we doing this?"

He answered, "playing a puppy gives you gives you a window into your animal self. your lizard brain, it's been called. It's a way to help you separate those instincts and the conditioning society has imposed on you. Understanding the difference will make it easier for you to accept the changes being imposed on you. I'm sure you know what I mean and also don't like all of them. This experience will make the changes less painful."

The next morning after exercises he took us to the shop. Wonder of wonders, the smith took out wrist and ankle chains off. He exchanged some impossibly angled light boots for our high heels. These had rubber soles and the heels must have been six or seven inches high and almost nothing at the toes. They were put on us as we sat on the workbench and locked to our anklets. Then thick, stiff, fingerless gloves were slipped on our hands and locked to our cuffs. Master had left our leashes on through the change. He had Rayna first step off the bench. She immediately dropped to all fours since the boots were impossible to stand on. She actually looked comfortable that way. Then it was my turn. I just copied Rayna and I felt agile. We weren't very good at four-footed ambulation at first, but we improved with each step.

Master led us around the corridors of the facility until we were comfortable with this new motion. He led us into a bath and gave us both an enema. Two actually each, until we were quite clean inside. He clipped Rayna's leash to a wall ring and put me down on all four's again. I felt his fingers lubricating my asshole. His fingers rubbing around and in my anus was driving me wild with arousal. My nipples hardened and my belly trembled. He slid his cock into me , stretching my sphincter hugely. I felt my arousal growing as he butt fucked me. His hands gripped my waist and held me tight as he rammed his cock home. I was on the brink of orgasm when he came. I felt his hot seed fill me up. I couldn't quite come. He stopped too soon. Shit. "Thank you, Master." He sat me back on the toilet and let me dribble out his spend.

Then he lubed me again. This got me even closer to coming. He inserted an inflatable plug into my asshole then blew it up with a bulb. He showed it to me. He also showed me a long flexible rubber tail. Then he screwed it onto the plug in my ass.

"Lagina," he said, "today you are a puppy. This is your tail. You are not to make any human sounds. Pretend you are a helpless, curious puppy and you are anxious to please. When a puppy is happy, she wags her tail. Wag yours for me now."

I shook my ass and I felt the tail wag back and forth. I smiled.

"'Great job. remember that."

He installed Rayna's tail and had her wag it. "Good job," he told her, "remember, no human sounds."

He took us outside into the fenced yard.

He had us practice puppy commands. We learned to 'roll over,' 'play dead,' 'Pee,' and more. The hardest for me was Pee. I had to get close to a tree and raise my leg high. High enough for those little chains to pull my labia lips open then squirt a few drops. Then I would go to another place and repeat. This was embarrassing. I guess it was another conditioning example of society.

He said, "I really like having you two on a physical leash. The symbolism is fantastic and the lust I get when you obey is better. Now though, I'm going to use your electronic leashes."

We both said, "What?" We had never heard about that.

"So," he said, "it works like this. There is an electronic leash built into you collars. I have the controller. I set the controller to 'leash' then a distance, say, ten feet. If you stay within ten feet of me, nothing happens. If you get further away your collar beeps. If you get three feet further, thirteen feet, is gives a mild shock. Every three feet further gives a stronger shock. Stay within ten feet of me and you'll be fine. If you don't obey a command, I'll give you a shock. Let's try it." He took the leashes off our noses and pocketed them. He walked around.

We tried to follow him closely but didn't have much skill on all fours. I heard and felt the warning beep many times. As I improved I didn't hear it much. He walked around the fence then back into the building. He went through the front door and I whined. I didn't want to play puppy in public. He had taken us out into the huge fenced compound. Free women, slaves and men could be here too.

He said, "Quiet girl and I'll walk slow. Remember, you are a curious, playful puppies. Don't think about anything but what a puppy would do."

He led us to a tree and said, "Pee, Rayna."

We both looked around. No one, good. She raised a leg until I saw her pussy exposed and squirted a few drops on the tree. She lowered my leg and wagged her tail.

Master said, "good girl."

Rayna beamed at the silly phrase. I knew what she felt. We may be just playing a role, but it felt so good to receive praise from our master.

He walked on and we hurried to keep up. We were getting better. He stopped by a bench and commanded, "Service me Lagina."

I knelt in front of him and started working my mouth to extract his penis. He had worn loose fitting pants commando style, so I was able to get him ready in just a moment. I licked and kissed his semi rigid cock until it was stiff. I sucked him all the way in, relishing the huge mouthful of cock. I moved my head in and out and felt my own arousal rising along with his. I tasted his pre-cum and savored the salty taste of my master. He came in a great spurt down my throat. I struggled to swallow it all without gagging. He pulled out and I cleaned him with my tongue, greedily sucking down all his cum I could get. I sat back on my heels and smiled.

He said, "Good girl. Great job."

I was fuller of pride than ever before.

He replaced his cock and ruffled my hair with his hands.

The man I had seen when I first woke up in a cell here walked up leading Mistress Katy on a leash. For the first time since I had first seen her, her hands were cuffed behind her back. She looked happy. The man spoke to my master, "Nice puppy. Love her tats. Does she know any tricks?"

Master said, "a few," then he commanded, "Stand, Lagina"

I rose to all fours, my bells clamoring like a church on Sunday.

"Roll Over."

I rolled onto my back then on over to standing on hands and knees.

"Lay."

I rolled onto my back.

Master came to me, squatted down and rubbed my breasts. It felt so good. My nipples got rock hard and I moaned.

He stood up and said, "stand"

I got on all fours and looked at master.

The man said, "Good puppy. I was so happy. The praise from a stranger hit me hard. I felt light stings on my ass and realized I was wagging my tail so hard it was whipping me. God, I was really enjoying puppy play. I was just feeling with very little thinking. I felt so free. I only cared about pleasing my master.

My master said, "OK puppy, go play. "

I crawled over to Mistress who was kneeling behind the man. Rayna followed me. I licked her breast and pulled on her nipple ring. She giggled and said, "Master, the puppy wants to play. May I?"

The man said, "OK. Be gentle she's only a puppy."

The man was holding a leash fastened to Mistress' nose ring. Her hands were locked behind her. I crawled over to the man and took the leash in my mouth. I tugged gently and whined. He looked at me and let go of the leash. I crawled onto the grass and tugged Mistress' leash so she had to follow me. She couldn't use her hands so I kept up a gentle pull while she stood up. She followed me on the grass. I stopped when my collar buzzed and rolled over the leash, forcing Mistress to the ground by her nose. I crawled up her supine body and put my pussy over her mouth. She couldn't get away with her nose held tight. I whined and spread my knees, forcing my labia lips open.

Rayna got the idea and put her nose into Mistress' pussy and started licking and sucking. Mistress squealed with the surprise intrusion she couldn't see.

Mistress got the message and started licking my cunt. Soon I was panting and juicing. I was so close to coming when my master stopped us. He unwrapped her leash from my body and took it out of my mouth. He said, Lagina, Rayna. Sit."

Mistress' master got her off the ground. He said, "She does know a few tricks. Good girl. And led Mistress away. She was blushing and her face was glistening with my juices. Her tongue was sticking out of her mouth. She drew it in and blew me a kiss.

Once again, I noticed my tail was wagging hard behind me. I looked and saw Rayna's was too. Master was walking a meandering path across lawns and through gardens. I was so hot. My pussy itched with frustration. I was still wet and dribbling from my loins. Several times I found a well shaped trunk or rock. I would hurry to it and rub my crotch, hoping I could masturbate to orgasm. But my collar would always buzz just when I got close and I would have to hurry after my retreating master. I was truly down to animal cravings. I only wanted praise and an orgasm. I was so hot. Rayna didn't seem so aroused. She just followed me around.

Master stopped to talk to another man and while he was busy, I crawled behind a tree and knelt. I rubbed my loins with my paws. It felt so good. I was so close to coming when I felt a shock. Master was calling me. I hurried to him. He looked at my wet paws and said, "Naughty. Bad girl. Stand. Stay." Shit. Caught.

I got three stripes from his whip. They hurt, but not enough to get off on. I was crushed. I slunk beside him when he walked. I was a bad girl.

My chagrin didn't last long. Soon I was trotting beside my master. Happy to be out in the fresh air with him. Everything was so new and fresh when seen from puppy level. I smelled flowers that were now at nose height. I rolled in the grass and stretched in the sun. sprung from behind bushes to touch master's leg. I trotted up close behind him and raised up to push him forward with my paws. I found a nice grassy patch in front of him and rolled onto my back. I spread my hands and legs and whimpered. He squatted beside me and rubbed my breasts and pussy. I was ready to come right then. I moaned and wriggled under his hands. He rolled my nipples between his fingers. They ached so good. I needed to come and I was close. He stood up and said, "playtime later. Come on."

We walked on. I was ordered to pee on several more trees along the way. I didn't see any more people. Rayna and I cavorted around our master. He was the center of my universe and I so wanted to please him. I blocked his path with my body so he had to interact with me. I wanted his attention more than I wanted his praise. He would have to give me an order, or touch me, or even step around me. He was always polite and controlled. I loved everything about him. But when he touched me, my heat blossomed in me. I felt unbounded joy. I knew he loved me and would care for me. He was my personal God and I glowed in his presence. I wanted him in me so bad. I wanted to serve him.

188

# Chapter 19 : Homecoming

"Good day, Minister," I said, "Rayna and Lagina are ready to be returned. Are your facilities ready to receive them?"

The Minister sounded happy to hear from me, "Good Morning Mr. Horn. I was expecting you to call this week. I'm glad to hear you have finished your work on schedule. Yes, we are ready and the King is eager to see his misguided family members. When can you bring them?"

"We can be there tomorrow morning, about 9, Minister. Shall we come to the capital?"

"Yes, Mr. Horn. We will be ready. By the way, the King would like you and you woman to spend a few days in the palace. He'd appreciates your suggestions and advice on handling of Rayna and Lagina, if you can spare the time?"

"Of course, Minister. Please tell the King we accept. I'll need to provide accommodations for my flight crew. We'll see you tomoorrow."

"Of course. Thank you and Good Bye, Mr. Horn."

"Good bye, Minister." I hung up.

"Katy, You and I are going to deliver Rayna and Lagina tomorrow morning early and we'll spend a couple of days in

Jedrah getting them settled in. Tell Manuel to have them ready to go by six am and I want to take their puppy gear, a milking machine, and their recordings please."

Katy smiled and said, "Yes, Master. Do you think our new slaves will like their home?

"I think it will be much different than when they left. There will be good parts and bad parts. We'll know more tomorrow, but its none of our concern now."

Master came into our cell earlier than usual. We scrambled into kneeling position as soon as we heard him. He put a leash on Rayna's nose ring and unlocked her tether from her collar. "Stand, Rayna." He led her out and down the hall. I stayed in kneeling position and waited. It wasn't long before he came back and got me.

He led me to a small room and not far away. Another man was waiting for us.

Master said, "Stand, Lagina."

I assumed the pose. The other man walked around behind me and Master took hold of my arm. I felt the prick of a needle and everything went black. The last thing I felt was Master picking me up as I collapsed.

Manuel removed the numbered tags from the girl's collars then the boxes were closed.

We landed in Jedrah about eight thirty in the morning, We were directed to follow a lead car. It led the airplane into a large hangar the was empty except for a limousine and two trucks. One was a cargo van and the other was a military truck with benches in the back. It was full of troops. All of the vehicles had flags on the fenders.

Master had allowed me to wear normal clothing today. A simple white sundress and white heels. I hadn't bothered with any underwear.

I watched as the soldiers took the two coffin-like boxes and carefully put them in the cargo van. One came back and got thee puppy gear box and put it in the van. Four soldiers rode in the van with the driver. Master and I rode in the limo with Mr. Haini, the Minister's agent. We formed a small procession to the palace. First the limo, then the cargo van, them the army truck. The trip was short and uneventful.

The palace was a big white edifice in a hundred acre garden. The whole thing was surrounded by a tall, high tech wall. Master said it was studded with sensors. I didn't see any. We were waved through a guard gate and the army truck stopped there.

The Minister greeted us outside the entrance. He and Master watched and talked as uniformed men took the boxes out of the van and carried them inside. We followed them inside and to a large, well furnished room. The boxes were opened and Rayna and Raime were decanted like two cadavers. The boxes were removed and two men picked up the two unconscious women. They were still fully chained and had leashes hanging from their nose rings. They looked small in the big room in the hands of big men. Master gave each of them an injection and had the men holding the lay them on the floor, face up in front of a couch. The Minister and Master sat on the couch. Master had me join them. It was a rare honor since I usually was not allowed to use furniture. In minutes they opened their eyes, first Rayna then Lagina. Master ordered them to their knees.

They looked confused for a moment then recognition and fear dawned on them. They stared at the Minister. He smiled, somewhat evilly, I thought and said, "Welcome home. You look wonderful. The King can hardly wait to see you. "Stand up, both of you."

Both of them stood. The Minister took hold of both their leashes and led them away. He called over his shoulder, "Please follow me, Mr. Horn, Katy. The King is waiting for us."

Master followed them. I followed Master, one step to his left, one step back.

The Minister led us all into another room. I heard him order them to kneel. When I entered the room after Master, I saw them kneeling in front of the King.

The King was seated in an ornate chair in his quarters. A lovely woman sat next to him. He stood up and greeted Master with a handshake and said, "Aaron Horn, this is my wife, Queen Adrienne. I remarried after the unfortunate actions of my former Queen. Adrienne is my Lagina's sister."

I could see the shock on Lagina's face. Her sister had taken her place. Adrienne was standing up and she walked over to her sister.

The King walked over and took Rayna's leash from the Minister and said, "Stand, Rayna, and don't move."

Rayna stood and went to her proper pose. I was glad to see she kept the smile on her lips.

The King walked around Rayna, running his hands all over her. Feeling her skin and all of her recesses and curves. I watched Rayna, nipples swell and get hard. We had trained her to easy arousal and she was reacting well.

Adrienne said, "Hello sister. I understand you are now called Lagina. Did you know that means 'Woman from Lorraine?' I love your new look. Its so appropriate for you."

She walked around behind Lagina and said, "Your hands are absolutely useless, aren't they?  How long are they kept up there?"

Lagina said, "T...They...They are always locked there, Mistress."

Adrienne said, "How wonderful.  You're completely helpless aren't you?"

"Yes, Mistress."

"And this is your lover, isn't it.  Or is it former lover?  Do the two of you still make love?"

"Yes, Mistress."

"You'll have to show me that sometime.  I've heard of your extraordinary tongues.  Both of you stick out your tongues."

I watched them obey.  I knew their tongues were extraordinary.  My work. They were much longer than usual with their rings prominently displayed.  They were thick and bulging with muscle.  I really don't know how they can keep them in their mouth.  They didn't look real.  But they were and I had made them like that.  I set out to make them both the best lesbian lovers in the world.  My guidance was to make them humiliated for the rest of their lives and this was the best way I could think of.  I was proud of making them unique and the best designed lovers of females ever.  I hoped the King and Queen would enjoy my design. On second thought, I was sure the Queen would appreciate Lagina. What girl doesn't dream of humiliating her older sister. She could make Lagina eat her out many times a day. How Lagina would hate that. It was probably the most humiliating thing ever to be a slave to your little sister. The girl you lorded it over because she was younger and smaller. Oh, the infamy.

Both the King and Queen's faces showed surprise then approval as they saw how their slave girls were both unique and useful.

The King said, "enough of that now, my dear. We have the rest of their lives to play with them. Mr. Horn you've done a remarkable job with my .. sister. No one would ever suspect this beautiful woman was once a man. Tell me about Rayna. Does she function well as a woman?"

Master said, "Your majesty, Rayna does everything a woman should, save have children or periods. We've started her on a milk producing program. She makes only about six ounces a day, but at the rate she is improving, she will make a quart a day in six months. That's about a young woman's limit. Lagina is a little farther along. We give Rayna hormone treatments to regulate her female functions. I've got her treatment program here." Master handed some folded pages to the Minister. Also All the cuffs and collars on them are permanent. They can be cut off them but would be useless then. Their chains can be unlocked if you desire. Here are their keys." He handed two key rings to the Minister. "Finally, both girls are trained as puppy girls. Their puppy gear is in a box where we unpacked them. Oh yes. Their collars have some imbedded control functions. They are powered by their body heat and will last for many years. Here are the control boxes. You can use them as an electronic leash or to punish them." He handed over the controllers.

The Queen asked, "How can they be punished with these remote controls?"

Master replied, "On the remotes there are red buttons numbered 1 through 5. If you push one of these the girl receives a shock. Higher numbers give higher shocks. Five will knock them out cold."

She said, "Minister, hand me Lagina's remote please?"

The Minister smiled and handed her the one labeled "Lagina."

The Queen asked, "You said one gives the smallest shock?" Master said, "Yes, your Majesty."

Adrienne held the remote out toward Lagina's fearful eyes and said, "How useful," and pushed the one button.

Lagina screeched and fell sideways, unable to move her hands and writhed on the floor, sobbing.

The Queen said, "Its very effective isn't it. Lagina, get back on your knees or I'll have to try number two."

Lagina struggled back onto her knees and adjusted her posture. Tears were still running down her cheeks.

The King said, "My dear why don't you take Rayna and Lagina into our bedroom and make them comfortable. I need to discuss some business with Mr. Horn. I'll join you in a few minutes."

Adrienne replied with a wicked smile, "Of course dear. Don't be too long." She picked up Rayna's leash an led them both out a side door.

The King said, "After you took those two away for your work, I pondered just what I would do with them once you brought them back. Slaves are not commonly kept in public anywhere today."

Aaron replied, "Most of our customers have secure private facilities staffed by trusted and well paid employees. Word of our graduates has never reached the public as far as I know. I assumed that was likely here."

"Yes, Mr. Horn, that was a tempting option and it was the most feasible for a while. It was not perfect because I wanted those two to suffer humiliation for a long time. Majid," he gestured to the Minister, "had a brilliant idea. You are probably aware that we are among the countries that employ the death penalty for serious crimes. After a little behind the scenes work several national and international women's organizations petitioned me to mitigate that penalty for females. I reluctantly agreed that I might do so in cases where the convict could provide some benefit to society. These groups wracked their brains for two whole days before suggesting that female slavery would be preferable to them over our standard method of execution - the firing squad. So female slavery for females convicted of heinous crimes, such as attempted Regicide is now our law. And, I might add, these slaves must undergo public humiliation as a deterrent to other females."

"A most ingenious solution, your Majesty. And quite appropriate for these two."

"I thought you would like it, Mr. Horn. It has the added benefit that I am now hailed as an enlightened Monarch who is improving the lot of women. This brings us to the business I wish to discuss. We have several more candidates for your program in prison. I would like you to look over their information and see if you agree these are suitable for your skills. Since these will come along at a rate of two to five a month, I would appreciate if your organization could give me a group rate for a long term contract."

198

" We would be glad to discuss a rate with your government. We will have to review our costs and see what economies of scale are possible without compromising product quality. Can I get back to you with a quote in a couple of weeks?"

"Certainly. Contact Majid when you are ready."

I was afraid he would be our negotiator, your Majesty. Your Minister has an enviable reputation as a tough negotiator."

"Yes, I know. I know that he will always do good for my country. Enough business. Come with me and I will show you some of the ingenious devices my staff have prepared to humiliate my new slaves. The ones in the palace are prototypes of the ones now in the downtown square."

Aaron replied, "Wonderful your Majesty. If you want to show them in operation we could take Rayna with us. Or would you like Katy to help demonstrate them?"

The King said, "Why not both. I would love to see Katy in some of these devices. None of them will result in damage to the girl. Just a moment and I'll get Rayna and Lagina I think my wife will want to participate too." He rose and went to the door to his bedroom. He entered and closed the door. In a minute he returned, leading Rayna and the Queen followed with Lagina.

It was a unique procession. The King led Rayna followed by the Queen leading Lagina. The Minister was next, then

Master and I brought up the rear. Master motioned me to walk beside him and I held his arm. We walked down a grand staircase and out a back entrance of the palace. We passed guards at every corridor and doorway. The King led the procession into a large hall filled with people. Many wore palace uniforms but there were twenty or so in civilian attire. A buzz of conversation stopped as the King entered and started up again as the two slaves came into the room. The King and Queen led the two slave girls to a low stage and turned to the crowd.

He said in a loud voice, "Thank you for coming to this informal gathering. You all know I was asked to stop our traditional practice of executing female criminals. I agreed and reinstituted slavery for females who would have been executed. These two females are the first two to be spared. They have been trained as sexual slaves and are here to be punished for their crimes by humiliation and public shaming. They will not be permitted clothing. The slave I am holding is my former brother, Ramalah. He has had his sex changed and is now female and called Rayna. The one my Queen is holding is my former Queen, Lorraine, who is now known as Lagina."

"They conspired to poison me and were caught. Jin, step forward."

A Tall, broad shouldered guard stepped up on the stage.

200

"Jin, you are a brave, loyal soldier. You are now the keeper of these two slaves. Ensure they stay health, live long, and are punished regularly. It is my wish they suffer humiliation and provide sexual favors to anyone who wishes to use them. I want them available to all the palace staff for their pleasure and enjoyment. Their trainers will be with us for several days to advise you on what they learned. Now, please take them to the new amusement area. Everyone is invited to help shame these two."

The King and Queen handed the two slave girl's leashes to Jin then led the crowd out of the room.

After we got outside we walked along a tall wall to a gate. A guard opened the gate and we entered. We had come in between bleachers on our right and the stage on our left. It was a low stage and there were a couple of wood and steel structures on it. There was a railing around most of the stage maybe twenty feet from the structures. Two uniformed staff on the stage bowed to the King. He said, "Put these two on the stands please."

Both staff said, "At once , Highness." Each man took a leash from Jin and led a girl toward the thing the King had called a stand. It was  steel frame maybe eight feet high and three feet wide. inside it raised three inches above the floor was a solid disc with two rings sticking up across from each other. A short chain was attached to each ring. Inside the frame at the top was a matching disc. A vertical metal rod joined the two discs   The rod had two cross pieces that could be adjusted up or down.  Each crosspiece had rings on its ends and in the middle. Hanging down from the top disc, a foot from the center rod was a chain with a four inch ball covered in stubby spikes.  Right below it, was a matching ball on a springy rod.

The girls were stood on the lower disc an a crosspiece moved right behind their necks.  Their collar rings were fastened to the center of the crosspiece.  Their feet were spread and the chains fastened to their anklets.  Their hands stayed locked to the backs of their collars. The spiked balls were adjusted to be level with their breasts and cunt.

Once the girls were both fastened in place the attendants activated motors.  The discs on each frame rotated in unison. The two frames were out of phase so when Rayna was facing us, Lagina was facing away.  They rotated slowly, maybe one rotation in twenty seconds.

The King explained what we were seeing.  He said, "This is the prototype.  The final installation is in the city square. Come over here." He led us to the outside of the railing. There were boxes below the railing.  He reached into one and took out a red ball.  He squeezed it and if was very soft. "This is a marker shot.  It has a thin waxed paper shell around a mixture of colored chalk in a water soluble oil base.  They are cheap and I provide them free to the people who wish to help humiliate and shame the miscreants.  If the thrower can hit one of the balls it will cause the girl a little pain, if he misses then the shot adds a little color to her. It washes right off, but I think it will add to her shame."

He turned and threw it at Rayna, who happened to be facing us. The shot went a little wide and burst over her breast, staining it bright red. "Try it as much as you'd like," he said, "in the city we have many young men that I think will like this game. When you are finished the staff will play with them until the shot is exhausted."

All of us went to the railing. There was a box of balls for everyone. I had played softball in high school and college. I was a fair shot with a ball. I hefted one. It was smaller and lighter than a softball. I took aim at Rayna's breasts and let fly. Bulls eye. I hit the spiked ball just a little off to the left and watched it smack into her left breast in her cleavage and ricochet into her right breast. The ball's burst sent chalk all over her chest. She squealed when the spikes hit her breasts. This was a lot of fun. As good as whipping her plus the marks it left were much more visible. I threw six shot and scored on a spiked ball five times. The girls jumped and squealed most gratifyingly. After we were ready the King announced everyone should try and said there were ten balls for each person. The royal party went to a raised box to enjoy the girl's public shaming. The King and Queen smiled a lot as we watched the spectacle. Some of the guards threw with great force and the girl's cries of pain were cloud and sharp.

I woke up in a place I recognized. I don't mean the room, but the decor of the room and the uniforms of some of the men looking at me. Despair welled up in my chest and I felt tears forming in my eyes. We were back in the palace at Jedrah. Damn. I hoped never to see this place again. We could expect only pain and unending misery here. It was nearly mine once. I saw Lagina laying beside me. Mistress and her master were sitting on a couch looking down at us. Mistress was fully clothed. The first time I had seen her with clothing. She was elegant.

There were several palace guards standing further back watching us with undisguised glee. Lagina and I were two beautiful girls. Naked, chained and available for them. I didn't move but Mistress and her owner saw I was awake. She said, "Just lie still Rayna until Lagina wakes up."

"Yes, Mistress."

I lay still and soon Lagina stirred. When she stilled, Master said, "Kneel."

Both of us struggled to our knees and faced Mistress. We carefully adjusted our positions to the standards she had set so many weeks earlier. I spread my knees as wide as I could, arched my back, thrust my breasts out, held my head high and my eyes on Mistress' feet. I scrunched down until I felt my cunt lips touch the floor. My hands were still drawn high on my back and locked to my collar. I glimpsed Lagina doing the same through my peripheral vision. I knew we looked good. We were lovely, submissive slave girls and I knew the guards were drooling. I didn't mind.

Lagina and I often talked about our new lives and our feelings. We felt the loss of freedom daily but escape was impossible. We were always chained so we soon came to accept our lives. We rationalized our helplessness as an all right thing, sometimes even as a good thing. We felt pain, but never more than we could bear. We had copious sex with many orgasms every day. We were taught to orgasm orally, anally, and vaginally. We could orgasm to the whip, the cane, or a hand. Applied to our bottoms, our legs, our backs, and our breasts. We could orgasm when a hand massaged our breasts or our pussies. We were milked daily and even that led to an orgasm.

We hated losing our freedom, but we loved being sex toys and having no responsibilities. The one thing we continued to hate was our humiliation. Once we both were people with heady power. Now we were submissive slave girls and must obey everyone we used to control. How grand that must be for them. I'm sure it will be terrible in the palace. Every guard, servant, and staff are now our masters and mistresses. Former friends and acquaintances can now whip us or fuck us at their whim. I shrunk at the thought of being in the power of these people who once thought me arrogant, unfair, and self-centered. I expected I would feel the lash and be forced to degrade myself daily. Death would be kinder.

I had not seen the third person on the couch until I got to my knees. When I saw him, I filled with fear and dread. It was the First Minister, he who had discovered my plan. I quickly shifted my eyes to the floor, but I had already recognized him. He was the one who discovered my plan and I was afraid of his wrath now that I was helpless before him. I couldn't see his face but I imagined his calm, happy expression. He spoke calmly, as if we had just returned from a trip. He said, "Welcome home Rama. I saw the look in your eyes. You need not fear me. You look wonderful. The King can hardly wait to see you. Stand up, both of you."

We stood. The Minister took hold of both our leashes and led us away. He called over his shoulder, "Please follow me, Mr. Horn, Katy. The King is waiting for us." Shit. Damn. Fuck. How can I face my brother? I had been taken away as his brother and now I was brought back as his slave sister. No choice. As always. What could I say? I had no explanation, no reason but my ambition.

The Minister led Lagina and I into the King's informal meeting room. It should have been mine. It almost was. Shit.

We had been taught to keep a smile on our faces at all times. This was most difficult as I was led to face the brother I had wanted to replace. I wanted to cry. I might be forgiven this once, but I didn't dare give in to my feelings. I knew I couldn't stop or even delay whatever my brother wished for me or Lagina. All I could do was endure.

I saw the feet of the King and a woman sitting with him. I did not want to look at him. I struggled to keep a smile on my face. The King greeted Master and introduced him to his new Queen, Adrienne. I knew that name. It was Lagina's sister. I had seen her before. She looked almost identical to Lagina. I didn't blame him. Both were unnaturally beautiful. The Queen went to Lagina and taunted her. I had heard that sister's often resented each other. Lagina must be dying of shame and fear to have her younger sister hold such power over her. It probably wasn't much worse than what I felt about the King. I'm his bitch for sure. Smile bitch.

The King walked toward me and took my leash from the Minister. He said, "Stand, Rayna, and don't move." I rose gracefully as I was taught and went into standing display. He put his hands on me and felt me. He inspected my nose ring, lifting it and rotating it, making sure it was a complete ring. He lifted my ring high so my head was tilted far back and held me there. I think he looked at the grommet in my nose to see why the ring hung so freely. He felt my collar, running his fingers around its top edge and feeling where my wrists were locked to its back ring.

He lowered my head and fondled my erect breasts, pulling and tweaking my nipple rings. He unclipped the chains in my rings and pulling my nose ring down, clipped both chains onto my nose ring. He ran his hands down my sides and belly and squatted in front of me. He used my labia rings to pull my outer lips apart and clipped the chains hanging from my belt to them. They held my labia lips open, exposing my inner lips to the cool air. This was good. I was getting hot, aroused. This may have been the man I tried to poison and replace, my nemesis, but I was trained to respond to any person who touched me as a lover. My body didn't care who touched its buttons. only that its buttons were touched. I felt my love juices trickling into my cunt. I was about to come from his touch. I was aghast, but he was chuckling. He said, "You are a hot bitch, aren't you Rayna?"

I said, "Yes, Master. I have been well trained." I was ashamed of my body's display of weakness and controllability. But resigned. I was a finely honed tool and I would respond to my erogenous zones, no matter how I felt about it. I expect Mistress was proud of her work. Shit again.

The King asked his wife to take Lagina and I into their bedroom. She led us in and had us kneel inside the door. My nipple chains were still clopped to my nose ring so I couldn't raise my head. She ran my leash between my legs and fastened it to my ankle chain so I couldn't rise. She said, "Rayna, don't move."

She took Lagina out of my field of view and I heard her say, "Lagina, kneel. Now let's see how well you can use that tongue. Come forward a little. Now lick and suck me off. Do a bad job and I'll use your remote again...Oh, yes, good...faster...higher...OOOH...Yes...more...AAAH...OOOH... ." I heard moans and her final squeal as Adrienne climaxed. "Yes, Lagina, your tongue is wonderful. Is Rayna as good as you are?"

"Yes, Mistress. We had the same training. May I call you Addy when we're alone?

"Of course not. You must maintain your discipline at all times or you might think me a pushover. If you ask again I shall take great pleasure in whipping your ass. I'm told you both like a whipping if its done right. When I punish you for cause, it won't give you any pleasure. I've been trained too."

"Yes, Mistress."

The King came in just then and asked the Queen to come to the party and bring Lagina. He released my leash and said, "Stand, Rayna. Follow me."

They took us into the auditorium and displayed us before a large group of palace staff. It looked like all of the non-essential personnel. He told them who Lagina and I used to be and that we were available to them for use. I saw several of my former aides and friends looking at me with undisguised glee. I would have a hard time with them. I could expect pain and humiliation aplenty from those I had once managed. Well, what did they expect from a Prince? I shouldn't expect any better I guess from people who would follow me.

He appointed Jin to be Lagina and my keeper, guard, Master, and everything. I knew Jin from before. I had tried to recruit him subtly but he was completely loyal to the King. The King took care of him and his mother after his father was killed in a military action. The King had recognized loyalty and capability and sent Jin abroad for education. Jin was a up and coming star in the executive branch. This was a smart move for Jin. It was good for Lagina and me. Jin wouldn't let anyone damage us. He'd probably bed both of us often. I wouldn't mind. I was good at that now.

They took us outside to a new installation. There were devices to hold Lagina and I and a grandstand for people to watch us be humiliated. Great.

A railing kept the people twenty feet from the devices. The King and his party lined up at the railing while the mass of people waited behind them.

Men in palace uniforms took our leashes from Jin and they led us onto raised discs with rods sticking up from their center. They stood me on one and Lagina on the other. We were facing opposite directions. He locked my feet wide apart and clipped my collar to the rod. There was a bar behind me so I couldn't turn. He put two four inch balls on in front of me. The one in front of my breasts hung from the ceiling on a chain and the one in front of my pussy was supported by a springy rod. The spikes were stubby things, not sharp. My hands stayed locked to the back of my collar. Useless.

At a word from the King, motors were started. The disc under my feet started rotating The two frames were out of phase so when I faced the crowd, Lagina was facing away. They rotated slowly, maybe one rotation in twenty seconds.

I watched the people on the railing pick up balls from boxes hanging on the rail. They were brightly colored in red, green, blue, yellow. Then they started throwing them at us. Several struck my legs and belly. They burst and coated us with some thick colored goosy stuff that ran down my body leaving their color behind. They stung when they hit, but softer than a whip or cane. Then Mistress hit the ball in front of my breast, driving its spikes into my left breast. That hurt as bad as a whip. Then the ball ricocheted into my right breast. That hurt too. I squealed in pain and shock. I was ashamed of myself, but I couldn't help it. The crowd was noisy, cheering every time Lagina or I got whacked with spiked ball and shouting encouragement to the throwers.

When the first group was done tormenting us, they stepped aside, attendants refilled the boxes with shot and the crowd surged forward for their shot at us. We hadn't done anything to them. My anger dissipated. We were here to be punished and this was some of that. Then the humiliation hit me like a blow in my stomach. I was naked and helpless. Everyone I had known was seeing me helpless and rubbing it in. Every colored ball that smeared color and pain on me was another affirmation that my power was gone. No one felt any fear or respect. I was truly and forever their toy.

It was all over in a half hour. Suddenly I was angry at these people. My breasts and pussy ached from all the hits they had taken from the spiked balls. Both Lagina and I were completely covered in colored goop. The guards ushered the crowd out the gate and the attendants hosed us off with strong streams of icy water. They toweled us off and took us off the stands. Jin took our leases and led us away.

Jin led us into a room I was unfamiliar with Its walls were bare and to my relief saw two milking machines like at the facility. Without any talking he strapped us in, put the heavy bras on us and started the pumps. It felt good. It had been yesterday we were last milked and I was full. He left us on them until we were drained. I hated to be so dependent on another for a bodily function. I still didn't make as much as Lagina, but it was enough to hurt if I wasn't milked regularly.

# Chapter 20 : Display

We were put in a big steel cage set in the middle of a green lawn in one of the courtyards of the palace. I saw it had a water phallus fastened to a bar. Just like at the training facility. There was a pile of dirt near a corner. I went over and looked at it. Beside it was a hole in the ground, six inches across and more than a foot deep.

Jin said, "Your toilet facility, Rayna. Cover your solid waste with a little dirt. Everyone is your master or mistress. Obey them or you will be punished. He pointed out a feature I hadn't seen before. There was a panel mounted to the outside of the cage. It was a box that faced out. He said In this box are remotes for your control collars. If anyone is displeased with you, they can push your button here to shock you. Annoy people at your risk." He walked away.

Over the next few hours several people, both men and women, came out to look at us. The first group of two women just wanted to look at us and taunt us. Lagina and I didn't want anyone to see us so we turned away from them. One said, "Come here and face me." Lagina and I looked at each other. It was an order from a free person. So we shrugged and went to them. We stopped close to the bars and the other one asked, "Is it true that you tried to poison the King?"

I said, "Yes, but we aren't those people anymore. Now we are just a couple of helpless slave girls."

"So you're here to be punished. Are they going to beat you?"

Lagina said, "We've been beaten regularly for the last three months. I think we are here to be humiliated, though I expect we'll be beaten some more."

One of the women said, I think you need more humiliation than just standing around naked in that cage. She pointed to Lagina and said, "Hold still." She reached through the bars and unclipped her nipple chains from her breasts, and pulled her nipples to the bars. "Stick your breasts through the bars."

Lagina moved up to the bars and tried to shove her breasts between them, but they were too close together. The woman saw the problem and said, "Keep pushing. I'll help." She used her hands to squeeze Lagina's breasts vertically and pulled on her nipple ring. She got both of them through. She wound the chains around the tightly around the base of the opposite breasts, then fastened the ends together.

Lagina's breasts were taut, round balloons and much too wide to fit back between the bars, plus the chains were outside the bars.

The other woman complimented the woman on her ingenuity. Then she turned to me and said, "Your turn.

Push your breasts through beside your friend." I did as ordered. I knew I'd be shocked until I obeyed. She soon had my breasts locked securely outside our cage. Now Lagina and I were cinched tightly to the bars with our ballooned breasts outside.

I expected a long boring wait and hoped I didn't have to pee. But they weren't done. One of them said, look at those clips hanging by their cunts. Don't you think they should be used too?

They both squatted in front of us and pulled on our labia rings. In a flash our labia lips were pulled open and the chains were pulling them not only open, but outside the bars. I had to press my loins into the bars hard to keep from being pulled apart. I asked, "Please don't leave us like this. Its unbearably painful."

The women both laughed and one said, "You deserve it." They both took pictures of us with cell phones before sauntering away.

Jin came out and examined us. He said, "That's a little too much." He released the labia clips and left us fastened to the bars by our breasts. He continued, "You probably don't know it, but they were kind to you. They could have whipped your breasts once they had them so well displayed." He went to the box and removed some small whips to show us. "These are available. They are designed for whipping breasts. I figured that's the only part a visitor could reach.

Now those kind ladies have made it easier for any other visitors. What can you say to dissuade that?" He replaced the whips and left us alone.

Three more groups of people, men and women alike came to share our humiliation that day. I had feared more would enjoy us. All of the twenty people in those groups enjoyed whipping our breasts. Lagina and I put on a great show for them. The dammed little whips had four knotted leather strands and they bit like a fanged animal gnawing on our stretched skin. The horrible things were well designed for though we were covered in thin red stripe that burned like fire, our skin was unbroken. We squealed and screamed and cried and moaned whenever the strands touched us. We stamped our feet and the bells in our nipples and loins jangled like a fire alarm. All our tormentors seemed to want to wring more noise from our wracked bodies than their predecessors. We cried for hours until at last Jin freed us from the bars and eased our tender breasts back into the cage. He put our food bowls on the grass and watched us eat. Then he made us pee on the grass near the waste hole.

His contribution to our humiliation was to take us on a walk. He put leashes on our nose rings and showed us our remotes in his pocket. He took us to the main gate and gathered a couple of guards. They opened the gate and he led us into the city to show us off. I could claim that this wasn't the worst punishment, but that would be a lie. I was helpless to stop or slow our walk. The nose ring is an extremely effective tool for controlling a woman. Jin held my leash and fastened Lagina's leash to the back of my collar, on the same ring my wrists were locked to. The two guards followed Lagina.

Jin walked slow and stopped to tell everyone who was interested who we had been and why he had two naked, chained women in tow. Our walk lasted more than two hours and he stopped every twenty feet or so to talk to another interested person. Almost all the people who wanted o talk were male. Almost all the women who saw us scurried away, maybe afraid Jin was taking women as slaves.

Several men asked where they could get girls like us. Several more wanted to know where they could have their women fitted with chains, rings, and bells like ours. Many of the men spat on Lagina and I when they found out who we were. Many men who didn't spit fondled our breasts and tweaked our bells. Lagina and I had to smile, but I could see she was as humiliated as I was. I had never felt so low since the day I learned my manhood had been taken away.

Jin took us back to the palace and into a bath. The palace was old and had a harem. There was a large sunken bath in the center that the King had refurbished for our use. Jin took us into the harem and locked hanging chains to our collars. Then he removed our leashes and freed our hands. It took us long moments to limber up our arms. They had been locked to our collars for many days.

217

He said, "Bathe yourselves and then use the toilet if you need to. There is a shower in that room," he pointed, "to wash your hair. Dry yourselves and apply makeup. I will return in two hours and take you to the King." He left and locked the barred gate behind him. I looked up at my chain. It was attached to a trolley running in an overhead track. Lagina's chain was fastened to another trolley on the same track. I traced the track and it ran around the bath and into each room. I looked like we could go anywhere the track went. I moved to Lagina and kissed her. It was the only friendly touch I had felt since the facility. It was wonderful. She kissed me back, obviously relishing the friendly touch as much as me. We finally broke and I said, "I want to wash now. I feel so dirty."

She replied, "Me too. Bath first then our hair? We can scrub each other's backs.."

"Sounds wonderful Lagina. Let's do the other places we can't reach too."

"Deal." We stepped down into the bath. Our new tethers were long enough we could get our necks into the water, but no further. It was going to be hard to drown in this bath. We scrubbed each other in all the places we couldn't reach ourselves. Of course we roused each other to high arousal and we wound up pleasuring each other to a fine orgasm apiece. We washed each other's hair and dried off. We did each other's makeup too. It was a lot easier than trying to do our own with our hands just barely able to reach our faces. But we finished in plenty of time and were kneeling in front of the gate when Jin appeared to collect us.

He locked our hands to our collars but this time he lifted our hands in front of us before locking them in place. Now our elbows stuck out beside our heads, Jin said this pose lifted our breasts and looked better. It was a welcome change from the usual reverse prayer position. We were just as helpless but there was less strain on our arms and shoulders. He didn't bother with the nose leashes either. He turned on the electronic leash function of our collars and reminded us of the ten foot radius we were allowed. We followed him up to the King's residence, our many bells jingling merrily. He knocked and when the King said, "Enter." He opened the door and escorted us in.

The King and Queen were both in the room. The King said, "Thank you Jin. Pick them up at nine am, please."

Jin bowed slightly and said, "Of course, your majesty." He left.

The King said, "Lagina, come here and kneel."

She obeyed, kneeling two feet in front of his feet.

The Queen said, "Rayna, here," and pointed to the floor in front of her. I knelt where she indicated.

The King said, "Girls, your breasts are well striped. I take it they were whipped this afternoon?"

Lagina said, "Yes, Master."

"The King continued, "Was it punishment for something you did?"

Lagina said, "No, Master. They were easy to reach and many people used them to make us cry."

"Rayna, was the pain the worst part?"

I ken what he meant. "No, Master. The humiliation bit deep and we will remember it longer than the pain."

"Why?"

"Master," I said, "it reminds me and your former Queen of our fall from power. It bluntly demonstrates that we are less than human."

"Then what are you?"

"Master, Lagina and I are your slave girls. We are helpless and wish only to give pleasure to you and our Mistress. We know you will punish us as you deem appropriate. We accept this and pray that soon you will let us serve you and pleasure you as we have been trained."

"Your condition was well earned. Do you think you have been punished enough for your crimes?"

"Master," I said, " only you may decide that. I know we erred grievously. We have been changed and well punished and now we would like to make amends by serving you. We have been schooled in the art of giving pleasure to both men and women. It would b a great honor if you allowed us to pleasure you."

The King asked, "Adrienne, would you like to have Rayna service you?"

The Queen smiled and said, "Why, yes, It would be a pleasant experience to have Rayna between my legs. I think we should both use these slaves of ours tonight before we couple."

"All right, my dear. Why don't you take Rayna in the bedroom and I will use Lagina here?"

The queen rose and said, "Come with me, Rayna."

I stood and followed the Queen. I heard the King say, "Come here, Lagina," as the Queen closed the door behind me.

The Queen slouched in a chair and pulled up her skirt. She had no underwear and had a fluffy blond bush. I could see her lips through her fur. I knelt between her legs and inhaled deeply. Her aroma was thick and sensuous and I longed to taste her fully. I licked her lips and felt them swell under my tongue. She was certainly responsive. I wasn't surprised. Her gaze at my naked, full-breasted body had never waver after I knelt before her. Her eyes were wide and full of lust. Now her nether lips swelled and parted s if by magic. I thrust my long, studded tongue deep into her folds, penetrating her love canal almost as far as my lost penis could have done a year ago. She gasped at my thrust and bucked her hips. I sucked as I withdrew and felt her initial contraction. I licked inside her inner lips and heard her sharp intake of breath. I forced my tongue ring into the top of her love canal as I darted my tongue in and out. Her breath quickened and she began to moan delightfully. I sucked her clit into my mouth and rubbed my tongue ring over it gently and she screamed in pleasure as she came. I lapped up all of her love juice. It was delicious and hot. I continued licking her loins clean as she recovered. Finally she pushed my head away. I looked at her face. She was unfocused and smiling in bliss. I waited for my Mistress to recover. As I watched her happy face I realized how good I felt. This was what I wanted. To bring joy to my owner. I had accepted I was a slave. I had even accepted I was forever female. Now I just wanted to give pleasure. I didn't want any more punishment.

She said, "You are very good, Rayna. I think you're better than Lagina. I shouldn't say it, but I'm glad you tried to poison my husband. You're the best sex toy ever. I think I'll reward you." She slipped off the chair and knelt beside me.

222

She put her hand between my legs and rubbed my labia. I had been trained to be instantly responsive too. I felt heat form in my belly. She rubbed me and thrust a finger in my pussy. I sucked in breath. Her second finger entered me and my belly spasmed. I was so ready to come. I needed to come. Her whole hand was thrust deep into me and I leaned back to give her easier access. She put her other hand on my collar and pulled me onto my back. Her hand fucked me rapidly and I came loudly and closed my eyes. I felt her when she pulled her hand out of my pussy and opened my eyes. She was smiling down at me.

She said, "That's the best kind of thank you, Rayna. Kneel."

I struggled up and assumed my pose. She took me into the bathroom and washed us both off.

The King came into the bedroom leading Lagina. He said, "I had fun, my dear. How was Rayna?"

The Queen said, "he was wonderful. I had fun too. Do we have to let them go?"

What? Let us go? What does this mean?

The King said, "Adrienne..."

The Queen said, "I'm sorry. It was just that she made me feel so good."

He said, "They'll still be close."

What was happening?  Where were we going?

The King said, "I know you have questions, girls. Just be patient and all will become clear. Everyone come back into the living room."

He led us all into the room. He indicated where he wanted Lagina and me to kneel and we obeyed.

He pushed a button on the arm of his chair and a servant appeared. "Real, ask Majid and Jin to join us, please."

"At once, highness."  He hurried out.

He said to the Queen, "Lagina was very skilled."

She replied, "That's nice dear.  So was Rayna."

He said, "I suppose they would bring a good price."

She said, "I'm sure they would.  Probably more if they gave a demonstration of their prowess before the auction."

I looked straight ahead, a smile on my face.  I knew they were jesting.  Probably.

There was a knock on the door and the King said, "Enter."

Majid and Jin entered.

"Thank you for coming, gentlemen, the King said, "Adrienne and I have decided these two slaves have been punished enough. Neither of you have wives or lovers. Both of you deserve rewards for your excellent service. I am giving one of them to each of you. Majid, you are now the owner of Rayna. Jin, you now own Lagina. There are a couple of provisions. You may make any alterations to your quarters you want for them." He handed a folder to both men. "Here are care instructions from Mr. Horn. Follow them. Particularly the discipline requirements. Also, the Queen and I will require the use of them several times a month . They are excellent sex toys. Make use of them. Here are their remotes. Take them and have fun." He handed them our controllers and shook their hands.

I looked at Majid, my new master. He said, Rayna, you are now mine. Submit."

I said, "Yes, Master." I lowered my head to his feet and kissed each one. Without raising I said, "Master, I am Rayna, your slave. I am your property forever and will obey you completely in all things. Command me Master."

I stayed down until he finally said, Kneel. Rayna, I am Majid, your Master. I will care for you and command you as long as I own you. You will obey my commands or be punished."

I said, Yes, Master.

I watched as Lagina submitted to Jin.

I followed Master out of the King's room and happily into my new life. I think my punishment is over. I was ready to serve. I knew I needed a master to serve. I wanted to serve him. I needed him in me so badly. I could feel my love juices dribbling down my legs. I wonder if he will let me use my hands to cherish him? As I followed him down the corridor he asked, "Rayna, I understand the two of you are trained as pet girls. Would you like to engage in some puppy play tomorrow?"

I would love to have the chains off so I could freely move again. I said, "Yes, Master. I enjoy puppy play."


The End

# Kindle Titles by Alan Horn

Total Control:

Total Control 1
Total Control 2
Total Control 3
Wage Slaves:
Submissives
Wage Slaves 2
Gods of Olympus:
Pony Girl Sentence
Consequences
Julie
Coffle:
The Coffle
Coffled Future
Coffle Cure
Laura's Key
Laura's Coffle

Pony Girl Dreams
Honor & Obey
Ensnared
The Love Ring
A Natural Slave
Humiliation
Iris

Bad Iris
Good Iris
Brave Iris

Printed in Great Britain
by Amazon

43259630R00131